Y.

John's Book

John's Book

by
Jill Fuller

Illustrated by Bill Toop

The Lutterworth Press
Cambridge

The Lutterworth Press
P.O. Box 60
Cambridge
CB1 2NT

First published in Great Britain by The Lutterworth Press, 1993
Copyright © Jill Fuller, 1993
Illustrations by Bill Toop

British Library Cataloguing in Publication Data:
A catalogue record for this book is available from the British Library

Printed and bound in Great Britain by
WBC, Bridgend, Mid Glam.

CONTENTS

CHAPTER 1

John was the first to hear the car arrive. The beam of the headlights swept across the bedroom window where he was standing shielded by the curtains. The throb of the engine stopped, car doors slammed. John waited to hear his father's excited voice: 'Come on, John. They've arrived. They're here.' He waited, allowing the realisation to sink into him. He would not hear his father's voice tonight nor any other night, nor so far as he could tell, ever again.

John stepped back from the window.

'Mum, are you there? They've arrived. Don't worry. I'm going,' he called.

He raced downstairs two at a time determined to be at the door first and before his mother.

His hands were clammy as he fumbled with the front door latch. He wrenched it open to see his aunt, uncle and two cousins standing wide-eyed outside in the darkness.

'John, dear. How are you?' His aunt's hands were on his shoulders, her anxious tired face scanning his own. How like his father she was, John suddenly realised. The tilt of the head, the expression in the eyes. He was aware of his mother's footsteps in the hall behind him. He mustn't cry. He mustn't cry now.

'I'm fine, Auntie. Absolutely fine. We both are, aren't we, Mum?' he said as his mother reached him.

'Teresa!' His aunt had enfolded John's mother in her arms and now Uncle James and his cousins were edging into the hallway.

'I'll put the kettle on,' said John trying to sound in command of the situation. 'I bet you could do with a cup of tea.'

He stumbled back along the hall to the kitchen, filled the kettle and began to reach into the cupboard for the mugs.

'Why have they come?' he muttered to himself. 'Mum and I can manage. We'll be OK. We don't need them.'

1

He poured the milk into the jug, put the sugar onto the tray and checked the mugs. He had absent-mindedly put seven out. He lifted one from the tray. It had been his Dad's favourite mug. John had given it to him when he was quite small and it had a picture of garden tools around it. Dad had called it his gardening mug and on Saturdays he always had his afternoon tea in it when they had finished the gardening chores. John fingered it gently and then lifting it up, pushed it behind the other crockery towards the back of the shelf. 'Visitors!' he said to himself.

The house seemed to have been full of visitors all that day since he had opened his eyes. John had awoken to hear his mother talking. She was talking in a low voice and a man's voice was answering, but not his father's. John had been awake in an instant, straining to catch the words.

'I'm sorry there is nothing I can do. There would have been nothing I could have done. It must have been over in an instant.'

His mother's voice then: 'If only I had woken. Perhaps I should have persuaded him not to go into work - the tension and strain...' His mother's voice had trailed off.

'You mustn't think that way, Mrs Symmonds. Now look, let me phone for the undertaker and later, when you feel more like it, you can contact them about the funeral arrangements.'

Undertaker. Funeral. The words had echoed in John's half-awake mind. He had jumped from his bed and in a moment was beside his mother. The next few minutes were confused in his memory. His mother's surprise at his presence, the doctor's quiet manner, the glimpse of his father motionless on the bed, his own hysterical fight to see his Dad. He had stopped, shocked at the sight of his father's pale face, and he and his mother had stood silent for a moment, stunned, before the doctor had persuaded them downstairs.

'Is that tea you promised ready yet, my lad?' said a voice. John, jolted from his memory, turned half-expecting to see the doctor but it was Uncle James. John was poised with his hands on the tea tray, lost in thought.

'Shall I carry the tray or will you?' Uncle James asked kindly.

'I can do it,' said John, adding 'thank you' as an after-thought. He liked Uncle James, it was only that, well, he couldn't really explain what it was. He only knew that he wanted to be alone, alone in the house, alone that is apart from his mother. Together, in

stillness, they could perhaps begin to absorb what had happened. But they had not had a moment alone, it seemed.

The day had felt endless and full of people. The undertaker, the doctor calling again, neighbours and the phone calls. The ceaseless phone calls. John knew his mother had wanted to make the phone calls when he wasn't there, so when she was telephoning he had made some excuse to be in the back garden. Then, creeping back, he slipped in the back door and listened. He could overhear most of what was said. Mum seemed to be perpetually on the phone. Dad's office, the bank, Dad's friends and relations and always the same phrase came in her trembling voice:

'Yes, I'm afraid it is true. Yes, a dreadful shock. No, John and I are fine. We'll be alright.'

'We'll be alright.' John clenched his fists and felt beads of sweat forming on his back. They would be alright, he knew. He would make it 'alright'.

'Are you sure?' said a voice. It was Uncle James again.

'Yes, quite sure,' said John taking hold of the tray. 'I've tried to make the tea weak how you like it, Uncle,' he added.

'It will be just fine anyway,' Uncle James said gently.

John walked into the lounge. Auntie Evelyn was sitting holding his mother's hand in her own. John eyed his mother suspiciously. She looked at him openly. She had not been crying, John observed. He felt fiercely protective of her. He did not want her to cry with anyone else but him now. He put the tray down on the table and passed the tea around. There was a silence, then Auntie Evelyn said, 'I'm sorry, darling. We're all so sorry.'

John could not cope with the pain in her voice. He busied himself, passing the sugar around and offering a biscuit to his cousins. Silence fell again, then Uncle asked, 'School going well, John?' John stuttered a few faltering comments about school life. He heard himself burbling out some nonsense about the school trip, his place in the swimming team, his progress in woodwork, pieces of news which now seemed irrelevant. All the time he watched his mother out of the corner of his eye. Was she alright? Would it be alright? How could anything ever be 'alright' again?

* * *

There was a feeling of timelessness as if the evening would go on indefinitely. John listened once again to his mother recounting the events of the day. It all seemed unreal.

'Any moment,' he thought, 'any moment someone will wake me up and prove I am dreaming. I will return to doing ordinary things, homework, riding my bike, listening to the radio.'

But nobody woke him and he only felt his eyes becoming heavier with sleep. His cousins, Hannah and Edmund, had long since been in bed. It was all such a squash with visitors in the house. He had made up camp beds for Hannah and Edmund in the bedroom at the front of the house where Auntie Evelyn and Uncle James would sleep. His mother would move into the spare bed in his room, they had decided. The room where he had seen his father this morning had been left empty. The undertakers had arrived in a black car and taken his father's body away. He had heard them moving quietly upstairs and then their clumsy descent. His mother had said that the body would be put in a special chapel until the funeral. Funeral. What was a funeral like? John had never been to one and had only seen the flowers piled up on new graves when they passed a churchyard or cemetery. Who would go to the funeral? What would happen?

'John, your auntie's speaking to you!'

John had been staring into the middle distance. Now he listened to his aunt, trying to focus his eyes on her face. She was saying something about it being very late, so sorry they had kept him up, time they all went to bed. Uncle James started to gather up the cups. At the sight of something practical to do John leapt into action. He felt better when he could do things, anything. He placed the last cups on the tray and carried them into the kitchen.

'Wash up, put out a note for the milkman, check the doors and windows are closed,' he muttered to himself. These were the routines of the night which he knew his father had always done. Now he meticulously followed the routine himself.

'I've done everything, Mum,' he called, opening the door to the lounge where they were still talking.

'Oh, John dear. Thank you,' answered his mother. She got up and laid a hand on his arm. 'Thanks for everything, dear. You've been marvellous - a great help. I'm just coming upstairs myself.'

'I'll get to bed then,' said John. 'Good night, Uncle James,

Auntie Evelyn, Mum - good night.' As they murmured their replies John walked up the stairs.

He could see his younger cousins curled up on the camp beds in the large bedroom. They seemed sound asleep. In his own bedroom he was soon in bed. He couldn't be bothered to wash or clean his teeth tonight. He thought he would stay awake until his mother came up. He could still hear the drone of their voices in the room below. Exhaustion crept over him and reluctantly he fell into a deep sleep.

CHAPTER 2

Back in their own home, Evelyn and James Murray were sitting over a late breakfast with Hannah, Edmund and John. John had travelled back with them, leaving his mother to make the final arrangements for the funeral which would be on the following Friday.

'What I think would be best,' said Evelyn, 'is if John and I go back to Teresa's by train tomorrow. Then we could give her a hand getting everything ready for Friday. Is that OK with you, John?'

John nodded. It would be good to be in his own home again.

'I'll leave you the car, James,' Evelyn continued, 'and then you can drive up on Thursday evening with Hannah and Edmund. You'll have to come on Thursday evening as the funeral's so early on Friday morning.'

'What *is* a funeral?' asked Hannah.

'What do you mean, dear - what is a funeral?' replied her mother.

'Well, I know there's a service at church and all that. But what exactly happens?'

The parents exchanged glances and John guessed that they were deciding whether to tell them or whether to end the conversation with one of those 'You'll understand better when you're older' remarks. All three children waited expectantly. John fingered the edge of the table. He half-wished Hannah had not asked. He was not sure that he really wanted to know.

It was Uncle James who broke the silence.

'Well, I suppose really it's when you say good-bye to the person you've known,' he said. 'It's a chance to be thankful for all that person meant to us and to share our sadness and comfort each other.'

Edmund looked anxious and fidgeted.

'What do you mean, say good-bye? Will I have to see Uncle Peter? Touch him or anything?' he asked.

'No. He'll be in a special kind of box - a coffin - the. . .'

'I know, I know, I'm not stupid. I've seen coffins before,' snapped Edmund, trying to recall television news flashes of funerals. The trouble was that on the television you only saw the people carrying the coffin or standing around in the churchyard. What actually happened? Dare he ask or was the conversation going to cause an upset?

His mother cleared her throat. 'You see either the coffin is buried or cremated.'

'Cremated? What on earth's that?' exclaimed Hannah.

Their mother paused.

'Well, when you die you don't really need your body any more and so it's taken to a special chapel at a crematorium and cremated.'

'Yes,' said Hannah, 'but what happens when it's cremated?' she persisted. 'What do they do with it?'

'They burn it,' said their father in a quiet voice. 'In a special fire. And then usually the ashes are put in a lovely garden or buried in a churchyard.'

Hannah and Edmund looked at one another. John looked at his hands. Hannah got up. Her chair scraped noisily as she pushed it back and she ran out of the room and upstairs like an animal running for cover.

Edmund composed himself. 'Do I have to come to the funeral?' he asked.

'Of course not, dear,' said his mother. 'But think it over. You might feel you would like to come when you've thought about it.'

'I think I'll go outside,' said Edmund, trying to sound casual. 'Coming, John?'

Edmund walked out of the back door and up the long garden of the Victorian house, picking up his football as he went. He walked right to the end of the garden which was hidden from the house by the chestnut tree. John followed him slowly and slumped on the ground against the trunk of the tree with his eyes tightly shut. He could hear Edmund slamming the football against the back wall of the garden as if he was furiously venting his anger and confusion and trying to understand what he had been told. At last, exhausted by the sudden burst of activity, Edmund slowly climbed to a special fork

in the branches of the tree. John could hear him rustling amongst the branches but he did not look up. The two cousins did not speak but sat in silence for a long while. Some time later, as if by an unspoken agreement, they came in from the garden and searched out Hannah. They found her standing behind the long curtains in her bedroom, hiding.

Edmund pulled the curtain back and gently curled the end of her long pigtails around his fingers.

'Hanny,' he said, using his most affectionate of nicknames. 'Hanny. I've been thinking.'

'Go away,' said Hannah, hugging the long curtains tightly around her. 'I don't want to know. I want to be alone. Go away.'

Edmund stepped back a few paces. Hannah was holding the curtains tightly up to her chin and from where he was standing John could see the tears slowly trickling down her face. He hated seeing her cry. He wished Edmund would leave her alone but Edmund went on undeterred .

'It's just I've been "chestnutting",' Edmund said, 'and I wanted to tell you.'

'Chestnutting' was their term for sitting in the chestnut tree and sorting out problems, arguments or anything else that needed quiet and time.

'From the tree you can see all the gardens up and down the road,' he went on.

'What are you prattling on about?' said Hannah irritably.

'I mean, you can see what everyone is doing and watch it.'

'How interesting!' said Hannah sarcastically.

'I've been watching Mr Sparrow,' said Edmund 'and suddenly everything fitted together.'

Hannah gazed out of the window across the roofs of the houses opposite to the distant hills.

'He's kind of spring cleaning the garden. He's raking up the leaves,' continued Edmund. 'The last bits and pieces that came down in the winter after clearing up last autumn. He's lifting them off the garden and the grass and putting them onto a bonfire. Well, I know what he does after the bonfire. When it's all cooled down he digs the ashes into the ground again. Not only that, but I saw that where he has cleared up the leaves there are new little shoots coming through. Tiny little spikes of green - daffodils or crocus or something,

I suppose.'

'Why is this supposed to interest me?' said Hannah. 'They always come through in the spring, stupid.'

'Yes, and Mr Sparrow always burns the old leaves and things and uses the ashes,' said Edmund. 'He's told me before - the dead things have to be cleared up so the new ones can grow.'

Hannah suddenly exploded. 'Go away, Edmund! I really don't know what you are talking about and I wish you would leave me alone.'

Edmund's shoulders drooped. It had all seemed so clear to him. He had hoped he could share it with Hannah and John and that what he had seen might help them to understand in some way. But now, as he struggled to express himself, uncertainty took hold of him again. He couldn't quite remember what it was that had suddenly seemed so clear and reassuring sitting in the early spring sunlight in the chestnut tree. Disconsolately he left them both and, closing the bedroom door, quietly went off to his own room. But John had heard and he had understood.

John stood awkwardly for a moment and then lay down on the rug beside Hannah's bed, pulling at the coloured strands of wool. When she was quite sure that Edmund had gone Hannah turned round. She came out from behind the edge of the curtain and sat on the edge of her bed. She fished down the sleeve of her jumper for a handkerchief and blew her nose. Then she rubbed her face over with her hands. Her eyes pricked and felt swollen and red. She tried to smile weakly at John but failed.

Life seemed uniformly horrible. Everything seemed to have stopped somehow and it felt as if nothing ordinary, let alone pleasant, was ever going to happen again. Hannah had adored her Uncle Peter. He, of all their many relatives, had been the one she felt closest to. Full of laughter, jokes and vitality, he had been extravagant in his love of his nephew and niece, lavishing time and affection on them. He had always known how to listen too, not like so many adults who only pretended to listen. She wanted to share her feelings of loss with John but didn't know how. Her heart ached for him and she longed to say something comforting but no words came.

Hannah looked around at her bookshelves. Books were her constant companions and she usually turned to them in need. Her friend Veronica had given her a book last Christmas. She scanned the bookshelves now and eased it out from among the tightly packed volumes. It was full of pictures and beneath each picture was a text from the Bible or a poem or a hymn. On the page opposite the picture was more writing. Hannah's mother said that she thought that Veronica's presents were pious and that she was trying to convert the whole of the household, but Hannah loved this book. She loved the photographs. She flopped down next to John on the rug. He moved over to give her space and they looked at the book together. The photographs were especially beautiful. They were in colour and were somehow very reassuring. Hannah turned the pages carefully. She hadn't looked at this book for some time. They came across a picture which Hannah had hardly noticed before, but now it was leaping out of the page at them. It was a picture of a fire: orange and yellow flames tipped with purple and blue danced upwards. Haltingly John read aloud the writing on the page opposite:

'Fire has always been important to mankind. When fire was discovered it meant man had found warmth, light and safety for fire could keep wild animals away.

Early man worshipped fire gods and even in Old Testament times the Holy Yahweh was made known to Moses in the form of a burning bush. One of the signs of the coming of the Holy Spirit to the early Christians was flames and fire on their head.

There is a very old myth of the phoenix - a bird which, when it feels it is near death, builds a pyre of sweet spices. The sun's rays light the pyre and the bird is consumed to ashes. From the ashes rises a worm which eventually becomes the new life of a new phoenix.

Fire is often used as a symbol of cleansing and warmth, of joy and celebration, and also of new beginnings.'

Hannah and John looked at the picture again. Did all fires really destroy? Could there be flames that were full of life and warmth like the comfort of a log fire on a winter's evening or the vitality of the bonfire on November 5th? Hannah sighed. She looked at John and they spontaneously hugged each other as if some new understanding had quietly come to them both. Hannah closed the book and tucked it away in its place on the bookshelves but neither of them forgot the picture or the ideas which had come into their minds.

CHAPTER 3

The day of the funeral had loomed large in John's mind. He was not sure what it would be like, how he was expected to behave or what would happen. As it was, the day came and went with amazing quickness leaving only blurred images in his mind.

The house was uncomfortably crowded, with so many relatives staying overnight and extra beds seemed crammed into every corner. Then there had been the early start to the day and the preparation for all the people who were coming back to the house after the service at the crematorium. Aunt Evelyn and his mother seemed to have made a mountain of food. Carefully arranged on plates in the dining room were sausage rolls, tiny sandwiches, scones and savouries all under clingfilm. Then there were six enormous dishes of trifle, and neat piles of serviettes, plates and knives. As John surveyed it all it looked as if they were preparing for some special kind of feast or party.

John's mother was at last satisfied that all was ready and went upstairs to change into her suit. John followed her. He fidgeted with his tie and shrugged his shoulders to get his school jacket more comfortable.

'Do I look alright?' John's mother asked, clipping a brooch onto the lapel of her jacket. John looked at her. Was she as nervous as he felt, he wondered? She had never asked him his opinion of her appearance before.

'Yes. Fine, Mum,' he replied, clearing his throat. Through the bedroom window he saw a large black car arrive.

'Come on, dear,' said his mother. They went downstairs and then walked up the garden path followed by Aunt Evelyn, Uncle James and Edmund. Hannah was staying at home to help a neighbour to make tea and coffee for their return. John sat next to his cousin

Edmund, and Aunt Evelyn and Uncle James sat either side of his mother. The car was roomy and splendid and John couldn't help feeling rather grand. He remembered accounts of funerals he had read in the paper and wondered if this would be reported similarly. 'Mrs Symmonds was accompanied by her only son', 'Amongst the other chief mourners were...' Immediately he felt guilty that such vain thoughts had crossed his mind.

At the crematorium, the floor was covered with bunches of flowers, wreaths and sprays sent by kind neighbours and colleagues of his Dad. John couldn't see the one he had chosen for his father. He had written the note on the card to be attached to the flowers himself.

In the chapel of the crematorium, the coffin which held John's father was on a kind of table. To each side were blue curtains and in front more curtains were drawn aside, rather like a theatre, John thought. He stood close to his mother and looked out of the large windows either side of the chapel at the bare silhouettes of the trees. The voice of the priest continued in the background, scarcely registering in John's mind. 'So here I am at a funeral,' John thought. 'This is what it is like.' He knew there were a lot of people behind him and he almost unconsciously got up and sat down with everyone else for the reading and hymn. Then the blue curtains pulled across in front of the coffin and it was over. He sensed his mother give a sudden involuntary shudder and felt quickly for her hand. She squeezed his hand tightly. Within a few moments they were being ushered back into the car and driven home.

At home all the relatives John had ever met were gathered together and many more he could not even recognise. There were neighbours and very many of his Dad's colleagues from work. John moved amongst them trying to be helpful, as his Mum had asked. He passed plates of food, carried cups to be refilled with coffee or tea and made what he knew his Mum would consider 'polite conversation.'

Once, feeling oppressed by the crowd of people, he crept upstairs into his mother's bedroom. To his surprise, he found Auntie Evelyn there. She was sitting on the edge of the bed holding a photograph framed in green velvet. She started out of her reverie as John walked in.

'I was just looking at this photo,' she explained. 'It's your

grandparents with your dad and me when we were quite young.'

John recognised the photograph. It usually stood on the chest by the door together with a photo of his parents' wedding and another of John himself as a baby.

'I wish I knew more about my family,' said John reflectively. 'There are so many relatives here I don't know.'

Aunt Evelyn put the photo back and looked thoughtful.

'Yes. It's important to know where you are in the family. Where you fit in the pattern of things. Who came before you, what they were like and what happened to them. I must see what I can do, John.' She got up from the bed with a sigh.

'Come on. We must go downstairs and help,' she said and she ruffled his hair affectionately.

Downstairs in the kitchen, their neighbour, Mrs Flack, was busy up to her elbows in the washing up. She lived next door with her retired husband and John had always found them kind and easy to talk to.

'You're going to be a regular help to your Mum, you are,' Mrs Flack said as John staggered into the kitchen with another tray of dirty cups.

That night when the last of the friends and relatives had finally left and John lay in bed, disconnected phrases from the day drifted into his mind. 'Do I look alright?', 'It's important to know where you fit in the pattern of things', 'A regular help to your Mum'. Then, out of the blue, some words that the priest had said at the service: 'Do not let your hearts be troubled.' Was his heart troubled, John wondered? Where did all this fit into any pattern that he could understand? And how could he help his Mum? He hardly knew how to help himself, mainly because he didn't really understand how he felt. John tried hard to pin down how he felt. Was he sad, lonely, frightened, uncertain? He could not decide but thought that most of all he felt relieved. Relieved that the funeral was over, for he was sure that tomorrow the feeling that he had had of being suspended in time would end and that life would begin again just as it had always been.

CHAPTER 4

The weekend after the funeral passed like a film in slow motion. John and his mother moved through familiar routines as though in some dance whose steps they knew by heart. Even ordinary actions like walking felt clumsy and awkward as though they were surrounded by some deep marsh of mud reaching to the thighs.

It was not until waking on Monday morning that the reality of the events of the last week hit John with any force. He awoke early in the morning with the feeling that there was a test at school and that he had forgotten to do the work. In his half-awake state he struggled to remember what it was he was supposed to have done. Then a rush of relief came upon him. It was the first Monday of the holiday - there was no test, nothing. Nothing. Then it dawned upon him. Nothing. He remembered and sat upright in bed with a tightening in his throat.

Downstairs he could hear sounds of movements. His mother must be up already. Without stopping for his slippers he slid out of bed and dashed down the stairs. Mum had put the breakfast bowls out on the table. Her back was towards him as she filled the kettle at the sink. John tried to compose himself.

'I'll get the cornflakes,' he said mechanically. His mother nodded. They ate their breakfast in silence. After they had washed up, his mother sat at the kitchen table and tried to concentrate on making a shopping list.

'I'll have to go into town this morning, John. We've completely run out of some things. I can't have been thinking straight last week. Would you like to come?'

John considered the idea. Walking around supermarkets never seemed much fun and he did not feel it would be right to ask her for a trip to the record shop. It seemed somehow wrong.

'No thanks, Mum. I'll stay at home and. . .' And what, he wondered? Usually he would have done something with his Dad, the gardening, clean the car perhaps. But what now?

As if picking up his thoughts, his mother enquired, 'But what will you do with yourself?'

'Oh, something or other,' John answered, trying to sound positive.

'I don't like leaving you in the house alone,' Mrs Symmonds went on. 'Won't you come? Just to keep me company?'

'I'd rather not. I might listen to my tapes or . . . read.'

'Well, if you're sure. I won't be longer than an hour or so. Don't answer the door, will you?' His mother picked up her basket and handbag. She checked the window latches, the dials on the cooker and did all the other things John knew she habitually did before she left the house. John waved her off as she went down the front path and then walked back through the hall and kitchen and into the garden.

Out in the garden John could feel the first real warmth of spring. The daffodils were in full bloom and although the branches of the tree were still bare, as he drew nearer to them he could see they were ready to burst into blossom and green leaf. John looked at the lower branches of the apple tree. The tiny light green leaves were folded around the blossom like some carefully coiled Jack-in-the-box ready to burst out when released by the first rays of spring sunshine. He kicked the tree viciously. What did he want with spring, with sunshine, with all the new life which seemed so incongruously around him?

He wandered down the lawn and stood absent-mindedly stroking his hand along the smooth grey bark of the walnut tree which stood at the edge of the gravel path. The walnut tree was nowhere near leaf. Its buds were slender and tightly closed as if it didn't believe in the warmth of spring and feared another frost. John felt the tightness of the buds. That was how all the trees should be, bare and wintery, he thought. How he hated the thought of the trees bright with blossom the colour of icing sugar. He wished the clouds would cover the struggling sun and discourage the opening buds. Turning, he caught sight of the greenhouse. Earlier in the year John and his father had sheltered in the greenhouse from the biting winds. Protected by the glass they had enjoyed the weak sunshine and spent Saturdays sowing seeds in the propagator. Later in the spring they would sow the outdoor crops in carefully hoed rows. John had always enjoyed doing this, fascinated by the variety of the seeds: The minute boat-shaped carrot seed, so hard to 'sow thinly' as directed on the packet; the crumpled seed of spinach, almost coral shaped; parsnip seed, so beautifully marked as if they were a miniature leaf, and tiny black turnip seeds, round and hard as a bullet. And all of them so dry and brittle. John would hold them in his hand, amazed that simply by putting them in the ground and waiting for warmth and rain they would grow into green leafiness and succulent vegetables.

If he walked over to the greenhouse now John knew he would see the seedlings in the propagator pushing through, green and fragile. He had always marvelled at the ability of the tiny soft shoots to push through the dark soil towards the light. Year after year the seeds unerringly made their way from the darkness of the earth towards the warmth and light of the sun. It had always seemed something of a miracle to him but this morning he was unmoved and disinterested. What did it matter anyway?

He picked up a handful of gravel from the path and flung it carelessly towards the greenhouse. The gravel pattered like hail against the glass. Suddenly John was filled with an overwhelming rush of anger. He picked up another handful of gravel and this time aimed a carefully calculated shot at the greenhouse. Then at that moment, he was seized by a desire to destroy the greenhouse and everything within it. He knelt down searching for larger stones. He found a sharp-sided flint and hurled it at the glass. A shattering crash followed. By now he was running around the garden looking for missiles and slinging them at the greenhouse with all the force his body could muster. The tinkle and crash of smashing glass followed each throw. Desperately looking around for something larger, John's gaze fell upon the rockery. He raced over and began scrabbling at the rough stones pulling and heaving to ease them from the ground.

He was panting and he could feel his heart heaving in his chest, but before he had managed to pull the stone away a hand grasped his collar and he felt himself being lifted up from the ground. He struggled and turned to see their next-door neighbour, Mr Flack, peering down at him. Mr Flack had always seemed tall to John, but now he seemed like a giant. His large frame towered above John seeming to blot out the sky itself.

'Now, just what are you up to, young John?' he said. His voice did not sound angry or even exasperated, just somehow puzzled. 'I just... I felt...' John stammered, his breath coming haltingly. His throat felt tight and he could feel his face was flushed. 'I don't know,' he faltered.

Mr Flack let go of John's collar and stepped back to look at the greenhouse. It was then that John saw with horror the results of what he had done. Two of the panes of the slanting roof had broken completely and some had been cracked around the door too.

'It's certainly a fine old mess you've made, lad,' said Mr Flack, stepping over to the greenhouse in three huge strides. Most of the glass had fallen inwards and lay in jagged pieces on the pathetic seedlings. John felt as if he had been possessed by some demon. What could have made him do it? He surveyed the damage with grief and regret.

'What am I going to do, Mr Flack? What'll Mum say? What will I tell her?' Panic began to rise in him. Mr Flack's heavy hand patted his shoulder reassuringly.

'Well, the first thing is to try to clear up this glass before your Mum comes back. And as for your Mum, well, I always think truth is the best course. But if you like I'll tell her what happened today and when you've sorted yourself out you can explain more clearly.'

At that moment the gate at the side of the house swung open and Mrs Symmonds put down her shopping bags on the step by the back door.

'John, I'm back!' she called and, seeing Mr Flack in the garden, she walked over to join them. 'Hello, Mr Flack. Why . . . the greenhouse! Whatever has happened? Oh dear! The lovely greenhouse and the seedlings!' she said peering inside. John hated to see his mother look so sad. He looked up at Mr Flack desperately. Mr Flack didn't flinch. His brilliant blue eyes remained steady.

'Who did it? However did it happen?' asked Mrs Symmonds.

'Well, some young boy seemed to go berserk in the garden,' said Mr Flack. 'He really went wild throwing gravel and stones everywhere. Fortunately I saw him from my bedroom window and John and I soon had the situation under control.'

'But who is he? Did you catch him?' asked Mrs Symmonds.

'I haven't seen that particular character around before,' said Mr Flack, 'Only someone like him who is a pleasant enough chap.

Somehow, I don't think that angry young man will come into the garden again. Do you, John?' John looked down and shook his head. Mr Flack went on, 'John and I were just about to clear up the damage.'

'But the plants! And how am I going to repair it all?' murmured Mrs Symmonds, her shoulders drooping.

'Well, if young John here could give me a hand this afternoon I dare say we could fix it up together,' said Mr Flack, rubbing his chin. A look of relief flooded Teresa Symmonds face.

'Oh, Mr Flack, I would be so grateful. But I must pay you.'

'Well, my time's my own so I don't want any payment for that, thanks all the same. But the glass . . . well, that's a different matter. Glass is expensive, I'm afraid.'

'Yes. Well, of course I'll pay for the . . .'

'No. I must pay for the glass,' John broke in. 'I must do that.'

'You, John?'

'Yes please, Mum. I'll explain later but I could pay for it out of my pocket money.'

'It would take all your pocket money,' his mother protested, 'and anyway why should you pay?'

'I think I would take up John's offer if I were you,' said Mr Flack. 'He's a good lad and I know the greenhouse meant a lot to him and his Dad. He really wouldn't want it to come to harm would you, John?'

Mr Flack caught Mrs Symmonds' eye and tapped the side of his nose with his forefinger in a meaningful way.

'Well, if you really think so,' she said, still mystified.

'I do indeed,' said Mr Flack. 'Now, lad, we'll get this mess cleared up first before anyone cuts themselves. Then I'll measure up what glass we'll need and after a bite to eat I'll get down to the DIY shop. Mrs Flack and I were going into town anyway.' He looked at his watch. 'So let's say I'll see you back here about half past three, and we'll try to put the damage right.'

True to his promise, at almost exactly half past three, John heard the side gate creak and in strode Mr Flack with a large rectangular shape wrapped in brown paper under his arm.

'You there, John?' he called. 'I've got the glass cut to size. Come on, we'll get this done before supper.'

John ran out of the back door and they walked to the greenhouse together. Mr Flack put a large cloth on the floor inside the greenhouse. Then, standing on an old chair, he began to remove the glass from the two broken panes. He carefully wiggled the pieces back and forth until they came free.

'Mind your hands, Mr Flack,' warned John.

'Don't you worry. I've got gloves on,' Mr Flack replied. 'I keep these old leather gloves for jobs like this.'

When all the glass was out Mr Flack removed the putty with a blunt chisel, then the two of them carried the broken glass and rubbish to the dustbin. Mr Flack wrapped the glass up carefully before he threw it in and clanged the dustbin lid down.

'Now we're half way there,' he beamed. 'It won't take a tick to get these two panes back.' Once on the chair again, Mr Flack put a layer of putty around the empty frame of the window. He carefully lifted up the new pane of glass and placed it against the putty. Finally, he ran a layer of putty around the edge of the pane finishing it off by pressing it with his thumb to leave the putty at an angle to the glass. John watched fascinated.

'Can I do the next pane?' he pleaded.

'Well, lad. You've been a great help already but lifting the glass at this funny angle could be a bit tricky. I'll tell you what. Could you go and make us a cup of tea? I'm gasping. And while you're in the house bring a piece of paper and pencil and we'll work out the finances.'

John ran back to the house, glad to be able to do something. Not once had Mr Flack grumbled at him or even asked him why he had smashed the greenhouse. It was as if he understood completely. In the kitchen his mother was making jam tarts, carefully placing a blob of red jam in each empty pastry shell.

'Mr Flack wants a cuppa,' said John.

'Good idea,' his mother replied.

'I'll take it out on a tray for him and me,' said John.

'You can have a couple of tarts each too. The first batch are already on the baking tray over there,' Mrs Symmonds pointed to the kitchen table.

John put the mugs, a plate with four jam tarts and a bowl of sugar on the tray. He poured out the tea and left a cup for his Mum in the kitchen. Putting a notepad and pencil in his pocket, he set off with the tray. He walked carefully, making sure he didn't slop the tea over the tarts.

'Perfect timing, John!' smiled Mr Flack climbing down. 'I've just finished. Now don't touch those panes. I know they look smeary but you'll have to wait till the putty dries out before you can clean them. My, they look good,' he added eyeing the tarts. John bent down and put the tray on the path. They both sat down sipping the tea and eating silently. John kept his eyes down. He looked at Mr Flack's heavy gardening boots and then saw his gloves lying on the path. They were leather and so old that the leather was stiff and hard. They did not lie flat as smart new gloves do, instead they remained in the perfect shape of a hand as if indeed a hand was still inside them. Mr Flack followed John's gaze.

'You looking at my old gloves?' he asked kindly. He wiped jam from around his mouth with the back of his hand. 'I use those for rough jobs like knocking out glass and so on. It keeps my hands smooth as my face,' he added with a chuckle. Mr Flack spread out his huge hands on his knees for John to inspect. They were rough and hard and strong. They didn't look as if they needed the protection of a glove any longer.

'I reckon I could do without those gloves nowadays,' Mr Flack reflected almost to himself. 'My hands are tough enough. They'll be glad to feel the air. Yes, I'll put those old gloves on the bonfire one day soon.'

John looked up into Mr Flack's face. It was old and wrinkled but somehow full of liveliness.

'You've been ever so kind to me today, Mr Flack,' said John. Mr Flack bent down to put his mug on the tray and gave John a friendly nudge on the shoulder.

'I don't know what came over me really,' said John.

'No. Well, we all do daft things sometimes,' said Mr Flack.

'I bet you've never done anything as daft as this,' said John, blushing as the recollection of the morning's events came freshly to his mind.

'No? Well, I have. And I dare say I was feeling just about the same as you.' Mr Flack paused. 'I've never told anyone else this before, John. Not even Mrs Flack but . . .' He stopped as if it was too difficult to go on and ran his hand over his face. 'When I was about your age something made me really mad. We were a happy family, Mum, Dad, three older sisters, a younger brother and me. I can remember it all so clearly. One day we were sitting around at the tea table and Mum said that she had something important to tell us. We thought it would mean a visit to our Gran's, a rare treat in those days as it was a day's journey and our Gran was a smasher and spoiled us rotten. Then we realised Mum didn't mean that kind of important - not a good important, if you follow me. Our Mum was having difficulty in telling us, we could see. Then she pulled out a letter from the pocket in her dress. I shall never forget. She handed it to our eldest sister Dolly and asked her to read it to us.'

Mr Flack stood up and turned to look across the fields that lay beyond the bottom of the garden. John thought he was not going to go on.

'What did the letter say, Mr Flack?' he whispered quietly.

'It was from my Dad. It simply said he was leaving home. He had been given the chance to go abroad with a friend and it was something that he had always wanted to do so he was going.'

'Leaving home?' John gasped. 'But what about your Mum?'

'No thought of her - or us. He just went. We never really understood and nor did we hear from him again. At first we couldn't take it in. We thought he would come back, write, arrive suddenly. But as the time went by my sorrow turned to anger. I was so mad and I didn't know what to do.' Mr Flack was clenching his fists unconsciously.

'What did you do? Did you break your greenhouse?' asked John half hopefully.

'I went down the garden to our old shed. My Dad was a carpenter - a wonder with his hands, he was. He had been teaching me how to use all the tools, how to make things, you know. We had been working together on a Noah's Ark. We had just finished the ark itself and were working on the animals - two of everything, you'll remember. It was a fine piece of work, the ark. There was a plank you could lower for the animals to go up and the roof of the ark came off so that you could see all the animals inside. We had varnished it. It looked a treat.'

John could visualise the ark and he could see from Mr Flack's face that even now, so many years later, Mr Flack could still see that ark in his mind's eye.

'Well,' said Mr Flack, 'I went into the shed and I picked up the heaviest mallet I could find and in a few moments I had smashed the whole thing into a heap of wooden splinters.'

John's eyes were wide. He was just about to say 'How could you do such a thing' when he stopped.

Instead he said, 'What did your Mum say?'

'She never knew. At least not until months afterwards. You see, the ark was meant to be a surprise present for my little brother Harry. When I had calmed down I realised how unfair I had been. So all that winter I worked every evening until I had made another ark and all the animals too. It wasn't quite as good as the old one but I had made it myself.'

'And your Dad? Did he come back?' John asked expectantly.

Mr Flack's eyes looked steadily into John's.

'No, lad. He never came back. But while I was making that ark the second time I remembered a lot about him. He had been a good friend to me - had taught me a lot of things about carpentry, gardening and the like. We had got on well. I began to think of him with affection not anger - tried to understand how he might have felt. There's a time for anger but then you have to put it aside - like throwing away these old gloves. I didn't need it any more.'

That night, John told his Mum the whole story of how he had broken the greenhouse, but Mr Flack's story he kept to himself. To his surprise his Mum was not at all cross. She only looked sad and held John close.

'Broken glass can be replaced in a day, dear. Broken hearts take a little longer,' she said. Then, for the first time, John realised that he was not alone in his grief and sorrow - that his mother was feeling it all too just like him, and if his mother was then perhaps Auntie Evelyn and his cousins were too. It didn't make the pain or anger any less but it did make John feel a little less alone.

CHAPTER 5

Despite the way the days had dragged, John was surprised when he realised that the Easter holiday was over and he had to return to school. He did all the usual chores which they always did at the end of the holidays.

There was the 'Grand Tidy-Up Of The Bedroom'. This entailed putting away all the books, games, tapes, magazines and knick-knacks which during the holiday seemed to accumulate over every available surface of the bedroom. Then came the 'Have You Got Everything You Need?' routine. This involved finding his games kit and his school tie, not to mention checking that all his clothes were named. It also meant a frantic scrabble on his desk to unearth pens, pencils, rulers and all the other paraphernalia without which he could not feel set to go.

Always at the end of the holiday there had been the traditional last family treat of the holiday. Somehow, goodness knows how, John's Dad would organise himself to have a day off a couple of days before term started. It was never the day immediately before term or they would have had to hurry home for an early night, which would spoil the feeling of freedom and the enjoyment of a last fling. They often went to London, sometimes to a museum or a trip along the river. Occasionally they went for a picnic in the forest or a trip by the sea. The outing somehow gave John the feeling of rounding off the holiday and helped him to set his sights on the next term.

John hadn't liked to mention the possibility of an outing to his Mum. For some reason his Mum had never learnt to drive and since his Dad's death the car had stood neglected in the garage. Outings by bus took a lot more organisation and John felt he couldn't ask for that. Then there was the question of the money. Would they be able to have treats like that now Dad had died?

27

It came as a surprise then when John found his mother sitting at the kitchen table poring over bus timetables and leaflets. She was leaning on one elbow with a cup of coffee in the other hand.

'Oh, John. I'm glad you've come in. I've picked up these pamphlets from the information centre. We must plan our last holiday fling.'

John hesitated. It would seem so odd just the two of them. Also he felt a strange and unfamiliar guilt at doing something so frivolous so soon after everything.

'I don't think...' he stumbled. 'Perhaps we needn't...' his voice trailed off.

'Yes we need,' said his mother firmly, looking up from her reading. 'It's a family tradition. Now, what do you think of these possibilities?'

She pushed a pile of leaflets towards him. He turned them over separating them into different groups. There were several pamphlets about museums: a regimental museum with weapons and uniforms of the past, a tank museum with a marvellous collection of tanks and helicopters. The pamphlet about the dinosaur museum looked good too. 'Fossils, skeletons, computerised and electronic displays' the leaflet read. Then there were museums with living creatures. The pamphlet for the aquarium and serpentarium was fascinating. It promised you could see 'deadly snakes, huge constrictors, sharks, crocodiles and alligators.' John gave a shudder of mock horror.

There were some pamphlets of castles with spectacular aerial photographs showing the whole lay-out of the castle and its surroundings. Finally, there were the grand houses. Houses with wonderful collections of paintings or silverware, beautiful gardens or outstanding architecture. John and Mrs Symmonds turned over each pamphlet thoughtfully. They discussed the price, the distance and whether they could get there easily. They looked at the various attractions of each and chatted about what they would both enjoy doing. At last they decided on Haversham House. The gardens and the collection of paintings appealed to Mrs Symmonds while John liked the look of the railway exhibition and the adventure playground.

The event planned, they decided to go on the Friday before term started on the Monday. 'Less crowded than the weekend,' said his mother, gathering up the pamphlets. 'Now, I'll put this timetable and the pamphlet on the kitchen pinboard. Then it'll be all ready for Friday. We'll try to have a nice day.'

John heard a catch in his mother's voice and realised how hard she was finding it to organise everything alone. He put his arm along the back of the chair.

'Thanks, Mum. Thanks - for everything.' Mrs Symmonds got up from her chair and made an attempt at a smile.

'We've got to try and go on, John - as near to normal as we can,' she said, picking up her coffee cup and moving to the sink.

Friday, the day of the outing, dawned cloudy and dull but as they packed up two flasks of coffee, sandwiches, fruit cake and apples, a watery sun appeared from behind the clouds and by the time they were walking down the garden path the day looked more promising. John carried the haversack with the food, while his mother carried her large bag which was always a joke in the family. Mrs Symmonds' bag was black, shiny and vast. It dwarfed her miniature size. It was full of pockets and each one had its own treasure inside. 'Your mother could meet any crisis so long as she had her bag,' his father used to joke. There was the zipped 'high security ' pocket. which held purse, cheque book, cheque cards and any tickets. Then there was a tiny buttoned pocket for the house keys. A medium-sized pocket held make-up, needles, scissors, buttons, thread and safety pins. A larger one was crammed with sticky plasters, travel sickness pills, anti-midge cream, insect bite cream, antiseptic wipes for grazes, and a vast supply of tissues. For good measure there was a pocket which contained what she called 'iron rations'. This was the only pocket which interested John for in it were always two or three small apples, a small packet of biscuits, a tube of peppermints and a medium-sized bar of Cadbury's fruit and nut chocolate. Thus equipped, Mrs Symmonds felt she could cope with any eventuality and invariably did. She always walked with the bag over one shoulder which, because of its considerable weight gave her a lop-sided look, and would-be companions were advised not to walk on her 'bag side' or they would certainly find themselves clouted by the formidable weight as she hoisted it up on her shoulder from time to time.

John judiciously walked on the non-bag side and together they strode off to the bus stop. To their surprise and relief, the bus did in fact arrive promptly on time. They checked their destination and clambered upstairs panting and puffing to the front seats. 'You can see so much more from the top of the bus than you can in a car,' said Mrs Symmonds appreciatively. It was true. John watched as the bus rumbled through the suburbs. It was fascinating to look down onto other people's houses and gardens, getting a bird's eye view of all that was happening. They watched as people pegged out washing and looked eye to eye with workmen in hard hats, perched on scaffolding. An old lady dozed contentedly in her front porch whilst her ginger cat sunned itself on the warm tiles at her feet. A poodle ran up and down dementedly barking alongside a lawn mower as his mistress cut the front lawn. Young mothers chatted concernedly over wooden fences whilst their toddlers conversed through an open knot-hole in the wood.

John usually only travelled by bus when he made the short journey to and from school. Then he was too busy chatting with friends and exchanging the answers to the previous night's homework to really observe the scene outside. Now he watched fascinated and wondered about the people he saw. Were they happy or sad, anxious or elated? He did not know and nor did any of them know what had happened to him and why he was sitting on top of a bus with his Mum instead of speeding along in the red Volvo which stood silently in the garage at home.

The bus swerved violently to the left. John steadied himself on the rail.

'We get off at the first stop after this roundabout,' said Mrs Symmonds. 'We'd better ring the bell and go downstairs.' They swayed along the gangway and lurched down the stairs onto the platform.

'Haversham House, Haversham House!' shouted the driver, calling back into the bus. Only one other elderly couple moved. The driver opened the automatic doors and they stepped off.

'Thanks very much,' called Mrs Symmonds but the driver was already closing the doors and signalling off into the traffic and did not hear.

Mrs Symmonds and John walked along the pavement until they came to a wide gravel drive. 'Park here for Haversham House' said a large black sign with gold letters. Their footsteps crunched along the gravel past a few parked cars and up to the main gates of the house. The wrought iron gates were slightly ajar and an attendant stood inside. 'Tickets on the left. Main entrance to the house straight ahead,' he boomed out. Mrs Symmonds turned left. There was only a short queue for the tickets. They could chose whether they went into the gardens and adventure playground, or the gardens and the house, which included the railway exhibition, or buy a ticket which allowed them to go to everything. They chose the latter.

Mrs Symmonds opened her purse and put the tickets inside.

'I'll take them, Mum,' said John. His Dad had always carried the tickets in his pocket and, feeling suddenly responsible, he wanted to do that now. Mrs Symmonds hesitated.

'You will be careful with them, dear. We shall need them to get into the house and they were quite expensive.'

John flushed.

'Of course I will. I'm not a kid,' he retorted and thrust the tickets into his pocket.

'Now, let's see,' mused Mrs Symmonds, looking at her watch. 'It's 12.15. The cafe is signed along here. Suppose we went and had an early lunch now and walked round the gardens afterwards. By then it would be about 2 o'clock when the first tour of the house starts. That way we'll be in the house early before it's really crowded. What do you think of that?'

'What about the picnic?' asked John, shifting the haversack on his back.

'Well, I thought we could have a picnic tea and finish off with the adventure playground. That way it doesn't matter what mess you get into as we'll be on our way home,' she added wryly. John weighed up the disadvantages of carrying the haversack against the advantages of being able to let rip in the playground before going home.

'It seems a good plan,' he agreed and so they turned down a laurel-lined path following the signs for the restaurant.

White-painted tables and chairs were standing on a patio whilst inside the restaurant the furniture was pine. It was self-service. They took a tray and queued up. For the first time ever John was conscious of the cost of the meal. Was it possible to choose anything? He thrust his hands nervously into his pockets clenching them open and closed. He couldn't bear it if his Mum hadn't enough money when they came to the till. He remembered her remarks about the cost of the tickets.

'I don't think I'm very hungry. Just a cup of tea for me,' he answered.

'Now you just choose a proper meal, John. I'm not cooking again when I get home,' his mother admonished. John scanned the menu suspended above the counter.

'Well, alright. I'll have a cheesy baked potato and a side salad,' he said, choosing the cheapest meal he could see.

'And we'll follow that with a large portion of apple strudel and cream and a Coca-cola,' said his mother giving John a wink. Apple strudel and Coca-cola were his favourites. He watched to see what his mother ordered. Ham salad, apple strudel and a pot of tea. He relaxed a little and began to relish the prospect of a good lunch.

After lunch they set off to walk around the grounds, which were huge. The last of the daffodils were still out and they wandered by the river which flowed along the edge of the parkland. They strolled slowly back to the house enjoying the sunshine.

'Just right,' said Mrs Symmonds as they joined the queue at the front door. 'It's just a quarter to two.' The clock in the courtyard in front of the house chimed the three-quarter hour and, as if by clockwork, the wooden doors swung open. Another uniformed attendant was standing inside and John could see there was a turnstile. As the visitors handed the guide their ticket he released the turnstile and they went in. It was soon their turn.

'Tickets, please,' said the attendant. Mrs Symmonds turned to John.

'Darling, the tickets,' she whispered. John felt confidently into his pockets with a sense of importance. His elation was followed swiftly by panic. He delved deeper into the pocket. He was sure that was where he had put them. But there were no tickets, only a mass of what felt like scrap paper. He pulled out his hand and opened it. There were the tickets all crumpled and torn. In his agitation at the restaurant he must have screwed them up and torn them.

'Now, what have we here?' said the attendant rising up and down on his heels. John felt the colour rising into his neck and then flooding his face. The queue behind him shifted restlessly from foot to foot. John gazed at the torn fragments in his hand. It would never have happened if Dad was here, thought John angrily. Dad would have known what to do. But how could he expect the attendant to understand that?

Then it happened. She seemed to appear out of nowhere. Dressed in a pale blue suit with a lacy blouse, her neat black hair swinging, she stood beside the turnstile. 'What's the delay, Brian?' came the cool voice.

'It's this young man's ticket, Miss Anderson. Just you look here.'

John caught a whiff of a flowery perfume as the person he took to be the official guide leant over. She picked the scraps of orange ticket from his hand, glancing up at his red face as she did so. She laid them down on the flat surface of the turnstile.

'There's no problem, Brian. Look. The dates are still clear. It's a ticket for today - just a bit crumpled, that's all. Let these visitors through. We're waiting to begin the tour.' The lever was released, the turnstile clanged round and John felt the gentle pressure of his mother's arm easing him forward.

'Thanks,' he murmured, looking up at the guide.

'No problem,' she replied laughing. 'I did that once with a theatre ticket myself. Only trouble was the theatre didn't let me in, so you can see why I'm sympathetic.' Suddenly John was smiling, the crowd around him was smiling and he felt his mother relax again by his side.

The house seemed to be all Mrs Symmonds had hoped for. She gazed in awe at its gracious architecture, the beautiful white and gold State bedroom with the painted ceiling, the incredible eighteenth-century furniture with elaborate gilt scrolls. Most of all she stood transfixed by the collection of old Dutch paintings, whose dark colours did not really appeal to John. John was only vaguely interested in the house. Isolated items caught his attention: A painting of a puppy by the feet of a young boy, a beautifully decorated grandfather clock, but mostly he itched to get on to the railway exhibition.

He was not disappointed. The exhibition was housed in a vast room and the train track ran completely around the outside edge. A background had been painted to represent the surrounding countryside and towns. There were tiny station buildings with porters and passengers with luggage. Around it several trains rattled and there were sound effects of steam trains whistling through tunnels and trundling along the tracks. A final attraction was that the whole scene could be changed from day to night by pressing a button. Diminutive street lights lit up, stars shone in the sky and the windows of the little houses beamed with light. John was captivated and would gladly have stayed there for hours.

It seemed no time at all before the tour was over and they were ushered out of another door of the house. Then followed a magnificent romp in the adventure playground. John swung from the ropes doing Tarzan impersonations. He scrambled up the commando net and slid headfirst down the slide. He walked across the pole bridge and swung across the blue inflatable pool which he pretended was a lake infested with crocodiles. Exhausted and filthy he eventually dropped down on the grass next to his Mum. She had the picnic tea spread out ready and John ate hungrily.

Going home on the bus afterwards he went through the events of the day in his mind. On the whole it had been a great success. He glanced sideways at his Mum's face. Perhaps everything was going to be alright after all.

CHAPTER 6

Returning to school at the end of the holidays was an altogether strange experience. During the holiday anyone who knew the Symmonds or came into close contact with John already knew all the events of the last weeks. He had not had to explain what had happened in any way.

Now, as he waited for the school bus to round the corner, John became aware that a new situation was presenting itself. Only a handful of his friends on the bus would know about his bereavement and few if any of his other classmates at school. What was he going to reply to the usual questions: 'Had a good holiday?' and the like. As the bus drew to a halt John looked up and could see his mates banging on the windows of the upper deck. Usually he would have given them a thumbs-up sign and clumped up the stairs, glad to be one of the crowd again but today a feeling of panic overcame him. He couldn't face their questions, let alone their sympathy. One foot on the first step of the stairs he suddenly decided to sit downstairs amongst the office workers and the shopping basket ladies. He swung himself into a seat flashing his travel pass at the driver. Wedged in beside a comfortably plump lady, he dug into his bag for a comic, buried his head and pretended to read.

At the school stop there was no hope of evading the crowd.

'What's up with you, Symmo? Putting on the class a bit this term, aren't you? What are you doing downstairs with all the grannies?' John tried to laugh and jostled along, giving off-hand replies to their questions. He did not want to talk about what had happened. He wanted to keep it a secret, a pain which only he knew about. But he was not going to be allowed that luxury.

In the classroom their form tutor, Mr Buxton, was already waiting. He had been new at the beginning of the year and was very young. Some of the boys thought it was his first job. Certainly he was incredibly keen and punctual, they had observed. He was one of those teachers who was always in the form room first, register at the ready, notices for the day prepared. They had never caught him hurrying along the corridor at the last moment, coffee cup in hand. Now he greeted the boys as they noisily entered the classroom and scraped back their chairs. After registration Mr Buxton gave out the notices.

'There is no assembly today but assemblies resume tomorrow - usual arrangements. A message from Mrs Armitage for those in her geography set - please remember your atlases today for her lesson. Mr Philips says the list of violin and piano lessons will be up outside the music room by break. Please check your times. Oh, and the cloakrooms have been decorated during the holiday - a warning to take care of the paint.'

There was a general sigh. Mr Grange the caretaker was not known for his understanding nature. The boys knew he would be examining the new paintwork like a hawk, ready to jump on any tiny scratch or mark.

'There's one more thing you ought to know,' went on Mr Buxton, 'and I'm afraid its very sad. . .'

The boys sat up expectantly.

'It concerns someone in our class.'

Everyone shifted uneasily. Surely no-one could be in trouble already? They had only been back for less than an hour.

'Now, you may have had very happy holidays but there is one member of the class whose holiday was not happy. Indeed for him it was very distressing.'

It was then John realised with great horror what was about to happen. Mr Buxton was going to tell everyone in front of him. He was going to announce it all. His mother must have phoned the school, John supposed. If only he could make a swift exit from the room but he felt rooted to the spot and could not even look up, let alone stand up or move. He felt the eyes of all his classmates turn towards him as Mr Buxton went on to announce that John's father had died.

'And so we all want you to know how deeply sorry we are, John, and that we are all here to help you in any way we can,' Mr Buxton concluded.

'Thank you, sir,' John heard himself say, but inside his anger was mounting. How dare anyone talk about it all, making him feel the centre of some drama. For a moment he really hated Mr Buxton and all his well-meaning and well-rehearsed speech. What did he know about it? How dare he suppose he could help in any way?

Quickly John got up. He grabbed his bag and pushed his way to the door striding along the corridor to his first lesson. What was his first lesson, he wondered? Geography - and he had forgotten his atlas. He turned on his heel to go back to the classroom only to bump into Mr Buxton.

'You left your atlas on your desk, John,' he said quietly.

'Yes. I know. I was just going back to get it,' John replied curtly.

'Here. I've brought it for you. I'm sorry. Really sorry. We all are,' said Mr Buxton. John snatched the atlas.

'Thanks - for nothing,' he growled, marching off again. As soon as he had said it he wished he hadn't. After all, Mr Buxton was only trying to be kind, but John wished people wouldn't pretend to know how he felt when he couldn't see how they could have any idea at all.

Somehow the first day finished, then the first week and the first month. John was bemused by the gradual realisation that everyday routine continued regardless of his feelings. It wasn't until a Tuesday in the sixth week of term that the routine was broken.

John had just got off the bus and was about to meander the five-minute walk home when a wave of fear enveloped him such as had never happened before. It was a great dread, a breath-stopping, horrifying anxiety, a premonition that something unbelievably awful had happened. Instinctively, John began to run homewards and, as he ran, his thoughts formulated more clearly. It was his Mum. Something had happened to his Mum. He pounded along the road, up through the small park across the last road and to the front gate. He clanged the gate to and leant on the front door bell. There was no reply. He pushed again frantically. Scrabbling in his blazer pocket he found his key. He opened the door and yelled 'Mum!' There was no answer. He ran down the hall and into the kitchen - no one there. Throwing his bag on the floor he ran upstairs two at a time and raced into the bedrooms, then the bathroom, flinging each door open and all the while screaming 'Mum! Mum! Where are you? Mum!' There was no one. Back to the kitchen he fled. Then at last he noticed her coming up the garden, a gardening basket full of weeds in her hand.

He banged out of the back door, his fear changing swiftly into anger.

'Where have you been? I've been looking for you everywhere!'

Mrs Symmonds put down the basket and took hold of John's shoulders.

'Why, darling, you're all red and flushed. What has happened?'

'I couldn't find you,' John spluttered.

'But you're early,' his mother exclaimed. 'You usually dawdle along. I wasn't expecting you quite so soon or I would have had the kettle on.'

She ferried John into the kitchen and moved to make them both a drink. Glancing down the hallway, Mrs Symmonds saw the trail of dirt left by John's hastening footsteps.

'Good heavens, dear. You were in a rush. Where ever did you think I would be?'

John put his head down. He felt close to tears. Tears of relief and tears of shame that he could let such an unrealistic fear take hold of him so forcibly.

'Can I have one of those chocolate digestives?' he mumbled, clumsily changing the subject.

John managed to avoid telling his mother about the dreadful fears which had gripped him as he had run home. Caught in the panic of the moment, his mind had run riot. Suppose she was to be taken ill, to fall, to hurt herself, even to ... John's thoughts went through every possibility. There was only him to look after her now, he reasoned. How could he go to school and leave her? There was only one possible answer. He would stay at home and keep an eye on her. He simply would not go to school.

The next morning John went into the bathroom early while he knew his mother was dressing in the adjacent bedroom. He locked the door behind him.

John stood in front of the mirror opened his mouth wide and pushed two of his fingers down his throat. The sensation was appalling. He began to cough and splutter. He paused. There was no response from his mother. John tried again pushing further this time. An odd strangulated sound came from the back of his throat, and he thought he would choke. He tried once again and this time felt so violently sick that he began wretching and burping and making fantastic noises. Mrs Symmonds banged on the bathroom door.

'John! What is it? Are you alright?'

John's eyes were watering as he turned on the taps of the basin and swished the water pretending to wash out the basin.

'I'm OK, Mum. Just a bit sick, that's all' replied John.

Mrs Symmonds banged on the door insistently. 'Open the door. Let me come in.'

John glanced at himself in the mirror. He looked suitably pallid and poorly, he thought with pleasure. He flicked the bolt of the bathroom door open. Mrs Symmonds burst in.

'Now, sit down,' she said, pushing John down onto the bathroom stool. 'What's the matter?'

'I just felt a bit sick,' said John. That was not really a lie, he comforted himself. He hadn't said he'd been sick and he certainly had felt sick the last time he had rammed his fingers down his throat. Mrs Symmonds put her hand on John's forehead.

'What did you have to eat at school yesterday? Was it anything which could have disagreed with you?'

John rehearsed the menu of yesterday's lunch: pizza, chips and salad, yoghurt and fruit juice.

'That should have been alright,' said Mrs Symmonds, looking puzzled and anxious. Seeing her worried face John began to feel rather guilty.

'I don't feel that bad, Mum. Honest. But maybe if I had a day at home, I might prevent whatever it is developing,' he said, trying to remember the reasons Mrs Symmonds gave when she kept him at home. To John's relief his mother agreed.

'You're certainly staying at home today. I don't want you chasing off after being so sick. Now, get back into bed and I'll make you a hot water bottle.'

'Bed?' John protested. He had not expected this. 'I was just coming down to breakfast.'

'Oh, I don't think you ought to eat breakfast,' said Mrs Symmonds. 'I'll bring you a glass of water to rinse your mouth but much better not to eat after an upset tummy.'

John was appalled. He was starving after all this acting and felt he could eat anything. But there was no dissuading his mother.

Tucked in bed with the hot water bottle he could smell wafts of the toast she was making for her own breakfast. He looked at the clock. It was still only 8.15. How soon would elevenses be, he wondered? But elevenses were not allowed and lunch, John discovered to his horror, was two dry water biscuits and a weak cup of tea.

'Much better to starve these tummy bugs,' his mother said knowledgeably. 'After all, you're not using any energy lying in bed so you don't need much food.'

By supper time John was famished and wolfed down the lightly boiled egg and brown bread which his mother brought him. At half-past eleven that night when he was sure his mother was asleep, John crept downstairs. He helped himself to two bowls of cereal, six biscuits and an apple. He had certainly been able to keep an eye on his mother all day but there was no way he could feign sickness tomorrow, he decided. For one thing his mother would be suspicious, for another he was sure he would starve. He would have to think of another plan.

By morning he had his plan worked out.

'How do you feel, John?' his mother asked as he walked into the kitchen.

'Oh, fine really thanks, Mum,' John replied casually. 'There's just one thing. Do you think I could have a flask with something to drink. I get really thirsty by break.'

'Of course,' said his mother 'but I don't know where all the milk has gone to. I could have sworn I had another pint in the fridge last night. Anyway there's enough and I'll put in half a dozen of these plain biscuits and an apple. I expect you feel rather hollow after a day of starvation yesterday.' John crammed his mouth full of cornflakes and remembered his midnight feast. 'By the way, I've put your excuse note in your school bag. Remember to give it to Mr Buxton. I'm sure he'll understand.'

John grunted. After breakfast he packed the flask together with the apple and biscuits. 'See you tonight!' he called as he slammed the front door.

So far so good. Now for the next stage. He waited at the bus stop, the next steps of his plan running through his head. Once on the bus he clambered upstairs.

'Hi, John! Where were you yesterday, then?' called out Tim, John's closest friend.

'Sick,' replied John, trying not to look Tim in the eye.

'Well, I hope you're ready for the greatest test of all time,' said Tim. 'The greatest test of all time' was a joke phrase which Tim and John shared. Mr Trench the history teacher gave regular tests. Each lesson he would remind the class of the forthcoming torture. 'Don't forget to revise. This is a very important test. I don't want any of you getting low marks,' and so it would go on. Behind his back the boys would laugh at Mr Trench's earnest lectures. The tests were never that bad. On the other hand, on the odd occasion when anyone had made a mess, Mr Trench had been known to fly off the handle. Extra work punishments and detentions were thrown in all directions. No one dared forget to work for Mr Trench's test. Risking Mr Trench's fury simply wasn't worth it.

John clasped his hand to his mouth. 'Tim, I've forgotten my history book. I was going to look through the test notes at lunch time.'

'Symmonds, you're a real fool. What are you going to do?' said Tim.

John had not sat down. He was standing grasping the rail at the top of the stairs.

'Don't worry. I'll get off at the next stop and run back. I'll be in time to catch the next bus and be there for first lesson. Tell Mr Buxton what happened.'

John clattered down the stairs again and jumped off at the next stop. He waved to Tim who was making faces at him out of the back window and set off at what he hoped looked like a sprint in the direction of home.

Once the bus was out of sight John slowed down. He had rehearsed his plan so carefully and so far all was going well. He would walk to a corner shop he knew and buy enough food for a snack lunch. He had the flask, the apple and biscuits so he wouldn't need much. He walked steadily around the back streets to the corner shop. The bell on the door clanged as he walked in. The corner shop was in a road John and his mother seldom used. The assistant in this shop would not know his face or his name but John had not thought of everything.

'Hello, son,' said the lady at the counter. 'What are you doing coming in at this time? Heron School's uniform, isn't it? All the boys from Heron left ages ago.'

'I . . .' stammered John.

'Overslept, did you?' the lady filled in sympathetically. 'And I bet you've rushed out without any breakfast. What do you want? Crisps? Chocolate flake? Or I've got some pork pies here if you're really starving.' Relieved by her friendly manner, John swiftly bought two packets of crisps, a bar of chocolate and one of the pork pies recommended by the lady. He stuffed the food into his haversack and walked on towards home.

How stupid, he thought, not to have put his anorak over his blazer. Still, an anorak on a warm summer's day would have been a bit conspicuous, he comforted himself. He followed a bend in the road and walked down the hill. John knew that the end of this road petered out into a gravel track. The track led down to a footpath along the river. If he followed the footpath along it went to the back of his house. There was just one field between the back fence of his house and the path. When he was younger his Dad used to take him down to the river with a net to catch tiddlers, John remembered affectionately. There were trees alongside the footpath which hid it from the view of the houses, but the problem would be crossing the open field to his back gate. He eventually decided to walk beyond his house, cross the field under the shelter of the hedge which ran from the back gardens down to the river path and then double-back behind the houses to his own back gate. At the end of all the gardens were potting sheds or greenhouses and, by walking close to the fence, John was sure he could reach his own back garden unobserved. It was still only 9.30 and most people had either left for work or were still doing chores inside the house. John reached the back gate. He glanced swiftly around to make sure his mother wasn't in the back garden, then lifted the latch silently and slipped in.

His planning was proving successful, John thought proudly. The garden gate was partly shielded from the back windows of the house by rhododendron bushes. Under cover of these John crept behind the shed. There was a narrow alley between the shed and the high back fence. In this alley John's father had put the compost bin and also kept any odd bits and pieces which he thought made the garden look untidy. John undid his haversack. He felt inside and pulled out two large dustbin bags. These, he thought, had been his master stroke. He cleared a space in the alley and spread one dustbin bag on the ground. The other he fastened against the compost bin to lean against. This way he had a comfortable chair. It was a bit like playing at being Robinson Crusoe, John mused. Exhilarated by the success of his plan he leant back in the sunshine. From this hideaway he could hear the noises of the house but could not be seen. If he crawled on all fours to the edge of the shed he could even peer around the corner into the garden. He listened intently. He could hear the sounds of the vacuum cleaner. Yes, this way he would certainly know that his mother was alright.

The first hour passed swiftly. The novelty of his make-shift home appealed to him and John fell into a reverie as to how he might improve his squat, bringing perhaps an old box for a table or a cushion to soften the ground. However, as the day wore on, he became cramped and restless. There was very little room in the alley and he dare not move about too much or he might attract attention. His legs became stiff and the mid-day sun beating onto the dustbin liners made them uncomfortably sticky and hot. He had divided his food into three piles: two smaller piles for elevenses and an afternoon snack, and a larger pile for lunch. But by one o' clock he had eaten almost everything and finished the flask of milk. He had only one rich tea biscuit left. He was dying for a long, cool drink and at one point wondered if he dared to make a dash for the kitchen, but he knew that was too risky.

At three o' clock he gratefully got to his feet and followed the morning's route back along the fences down by the hedge and by the river path once more. He walked along the roadway back to his own street and rang the bell.

'Early tonight, John,' remarked his mother.

'I ran fast and managed to catch the early bus,' John lied.

'Got much homework?'

'Er . . . no. None at all, thank goodness.' John remembered the history test and Mr Trench. He wondered how he could explain his absence to Tim and how he was going to manage to truant again tomorrow. The trouble with truanting was that he had to leave at the time his mother expected him to leave. Then automatically he ran into friends who might report that they had seen him on their way to school. If he was away a friend like Tim was sure to ring up in the evening to ask where he had been. What if his mother should answer the phone first? What then? John turned the problem over in his mind. He would have to think of another excuse for Tim tomorrow.

* * *

As the bus screeched to a standstill the following morning John could see Tim making thumbs-down signals to him from the back seat.

'You're really for the high jump today, John-boy. Where did you get to? Mr Trench flipped his lid. Mr Buxton was a bit put out too at afternoon registration.'

John felt concerned. What if Mr Buxton should phone home and ask where he had been?

'Did you tell Mr Buxton that I'd been sick on Wednesday?' asked John.

'You bet. But he couldn't understand why you were away Thursday as well. Especially as you'd told me you were catching the next bus. Where were you then?'

'Well, when I got home for the history book I threw up again. I suppose I hadn't really got over the bug,' said John.

'Bit daft coming back today on a Friday,' said Tim. 'I would have stayed at home. Given old Trench a chance to forget the test you missed over the weekend. He'll murder you first lesson today you'll see.'

'I won't be in school until after first lesson,' said John. Tim looked puzzled.

'What you going to do then? Go to sick bay? Throw up again? That's a good idea.'

'Don't be daft, Tim,' said John. He wasn't used to deceiving anybody, let alone his best friend, so he looked out of the window as he answered. 'Got this dental appointment. A filling's come out in my back tooth.' He pointed to the back of his mouth with his finger. 'I'm going into town for the appointment before I come into school.'

The bus route went through the town centre and up the hill the other side to the Heron School. John planned to get off in the centre and then walk back to his hide-out. It would be a longer walk but at least it meant Tim had a story he could relay to Mr Buxton. Tim looked doubtful.

'What time do you reckon you'll be back?' he asked.

'Easily by ten. But don't worry if it's later. You know what dentists are like. Our dentist is always late. You will explain to Mr Buxton won't you?'

'OK,' said Tim slowly. 'But honestly, John, you'd better make it by eleven. Mr Buxton was really concerned yesterday.'

By now the bus had reached the town centre.

'Thanks, Tim. See you later,' called John.

He got off the bus and walked across the market square. The stalls were already up: Greengrocers stalls laden with fruit and vegetables; the fabric stall with rolls of cotton and polyester, printed and plain, piled on the trestles; the fishmonger's at the edge of the market; the clothes stalls with jackets and skirts swinging from the rails. John turned down a side street. He knew how to cut back along the bus route and he was soon away from the market square and into the suburban roads again. What he had not reckoned with was the weather. As he strode along the road, without any warning the clouds above burst and torrential rain poured down. John had never seen such rain. It bounced off the pavements and gurgled down the gutters. He looked around for shelter. He wished he had stayed in the centre of town. There he could have taken cover in a shop doorway or even run into the library, but here amongst the rows of residential houses there was nowhere to hide from the relentless rain. There was not a bus shelter or telephone kiosk in sight. He could not knock at a stranger's door and ask for shelter, besides they would be suspicious, ask him why he wasn't at school.

John was soaked through. He felt the dampness of his blazer and his shirt was clinging to his shoulders. The rain was trickling off his face and saturated hair, and running down his neck while his trousers were flapping wetly around his ankles. He couldn't remember ever being so wet. One thing was certain. Even if the rain stopped he couldn't repeat yesterday's plan. There was no way he could sit in his hide-out soaked through like this.

John turned in his tracks. The town was the only place he could find shelter. As he ran back towards the market square, an idea came to him. In one of the side streets was a launderette called The Washing Well. John had noticed the name before. He had taken some of his own money to buy his lunch. Perhaps he would have enough to dry out his clothes in the drier. He turned right into the street and splashed along looking for the sign. He pushed open the door, glad to be out of the downpour. He stood on the doormat, water streaming from him. The launderette was empty. It must be because it's still early, John reasoned. He looked around. His mother had a washing machine at home and so he had never been to a launderette before. There were washing machines all along one side of the room, driers along the other. On top of the machines were empty upturned washing baskets of red, blue and yellow plastic. They had The Washing Well written in felt tip along the rim. Next to the driers was a machine which dispensed washing powder in cups and another which was for tea or coffee. What should he do? John remembered an advert he had seen on the television: a man walked into the launderette, stripped off his clothes, put them all in the machine and then sat down in his underpants with a book to wait, while everyone watched him admiringly. It all looked so easy on the TV, but John wasn't so sure. True, there was no one in the launderette but the door was glass and anyone could see in easily. Just then there was a click as a door at the back of the room which John hadn't noticed before opened. A tall thin woman in pink and cream overalls stood in the doorway.

'I thought I heard someone come in,' she said. 'You leaving your Mum's washing here to be done?'

John looked about awkwardly. 'Well, no . . . I . . .'

'You've not been messing about with my machines, have you?' she asked threateningly. 'Sick and tired, I am, of some of you youngsters. Last week some fool filled the soap dispenser on all the machines with liquid soap. Not suitable for these automatic machines, it isn't. I had bubbles and water all over the place. Then the week before someone put a dollop of red powder paint inside the drum. Some poor gent's underwear came out bright pink. He wasn't at all amused, I can tell you.'

John tried not to smile as he imagined the flood of bubbles and the pink underpants.

'No, no. I haven't touched the machines. It's just . . . Could I use the driers? You see, I've got soaked through.'

'Soaked through? Raining, is it?' She glanced outside for the first time.

'Can't hear or see much at all from my back room,' she continued, nodding towards the door at the back from which she had emerged. 'Use the driers! You can't use the driers unless you've used the washers.' She pointed to a large notice printed in red block capitals hanging above the drying machine. 'These driers are for the exclusive use of customers using the washing machines,' she read aloud. John shivered involuntarily and looked down at the ever-increasing pool of water at his feet. He was beginning to feel thoroughly uncomfortable.

'Anyway how did you manage to get that wet?' the woman went on unsympathetically. At that moment the door of the launderette clanged open and a tiny lady pulling what seemed a vast trolley laden with a yellow plastic bag trundled in. She was wearing a pink mac and wielding a huge multi-coloured golf umbrella which nearly enveloped her.

'Why, Aggie. What a morning!' she exclaimed. John instinctively went to help. He heaved the trolley over the threshold and shut the door against the driving rain.

'Well, thank you,' said the tiny lady.

'Morning, Ethel,' said the launderette assistant.

'You poor soul!' said the lady called Ethel, looking at John. 'You've got caught in that downpour just like me. Just look at the child, Aggie! He's soaked.'

Aggie the launderette lady glowered at John.

'What he needs is to get out of those wet clothes and to put them in the drier, he does,' continued the lady called Ethel. Aggie sniffed. 'Could catch his death of cold staying in these wet clothes, he could,' Ethel persisted.

'I've got some money for the drier,' said John, feeling that might soften Aggie's attitude.

'Hmm,' muttered Aggie unimpressed. 'But where are you meant to sit then? I can hardly have naked young men sitting in my launderette. It's against the rules.'

But Ethel was not so easily daunted. She took a bright blue clothes basket and tipped the copious contents of her yellow plastic bag into it. Pillow cases, underwear, tablecloths, blouses, shirts fell in disarray into the basket. Ethel rummaged about.

'This is what he needs,' she announced triumphantly, pulling out a huge beach towel with palm trees in psychedelic colours on a navy background. 'He can wrap himself up in this.'

John looked at Aggie. Her mouth twitched. She even smiled a bit. 'Well, I give in. Go into my back room and change. Here, take this basket with you for your clothes and then come out with the towel round you. I don't suppose I'll have many customers in this weather so no one will see you.'

John grabbed the basket. He changed in Aggie's rest room. Looking around at the tiny space she had to inhabit each day he could understand her irritability. There was a hard chair, a small table and an electric kettle. The minute window was high up in the wall. She would not be able to see outside at all. On the table sat a bottle of milk, two mugs and a tin box of biscuits. He took out the contents of his blazer and trouser pockets and put them in his school bag. He laid his vest, shirt, tie, pullover, trousers and blazer carefully in the basket. He draped the towel around him in such a way as to achieve maximum coverage and then carried the basket to the door of Aggie's room. At his appearance Aggie and Ethel fell about in helpless laughter.

'You'd better sit up this end away from the door,' said Aggie. 'Come here, I'll put the clothes in the drier.' She took the basket and John's money. Soon the drier was spinning around and John could see his clothes hurtling about through the glass porthole. At the end of one session they were still damp but Aggie had warmed to John and put them in again twice more without further payment. She fiddled about with the switch of the machine.

'Don't you tell anyone what I've done,' she said wagging her finger at John. 'But I can't let you go out in those soaking clothes.'

'Certainly not,' agreed Ethel, winking at John behind Aggie's back. Eventually Aggie and Ethel were satisfied that the clothes were dry and John was dispatched to the back room again to get dressed. The clothed were crumpled but warm. They smelt rather like a dog's coat when it's been caught in a shower.

John dressed, picked up his bag and came back into the launderette.

'I really am ever so grateful,' he said trying to smile a bit. Aggie and Ethel were by now sitting together enjoying a cup of tea.

'Now, just you hurry off to school,' said Ethel, smiling and nodding.

'Well, thanks again,' said John.

He closed the launderette door and stepped out on to the glistening pavement. The rain had stopped, he noticed with relief. Seeing the women drinking their tea had made him realise how hungry and thirsty he felt. He felt in his pocket. He had just about enough money left for a hot drink and something to eat. There was a cafe on the corner of the street. The windows had wooden poles half way up from which hung net curtains. Inside it looked quiet but not too posh or expensive, John decided. There was a hand-written menu inside a wooden frame hanging by the door. John examined it. Tea 50p, Coffee 60p, Toasted tea cake 45p, Scone and butter 40p. Then it listed snacks and hot meals. John felt in his pocket and checked his money. He could afford a cup of tea and a toasted tea cake. He moved towards the door but as he turned he saw something which caused panic to seize him. There running towards him was Mr Buxton. John started to dart into the cafe but a loud voice called out,

'John. John Symmonds. Stay where you are.'

In no time at all Mr Buxton was beside him, followed closely by a crowd of boys from Heron School, Miss Jonson and two parents. It seemed that the cafe had been the meeting place for the group who had been in Wimbury collecting information for a project about the market. The boys were not from John's year so although they gave him inquisitive glances they did not know him well enough to ask difficult questions. Mr Buxton was talking quietly to Miss Jonson. He held up his hand and spoke to the boys.

'Now, listen all of you. Miss Jonson is taking you all back to school now. Mrs Morgan and Mrs Williams are going with you. That means five boys to each adult. Get yourselves into groups of five quickly. I expect you to be sensible and responsible. When you get back to school, leave your project folders in my locker and go straight back to your ordinary lesson. If you hurry up you could still be in time for break. I'll see you all at this afternoon's lesson and we'll go over the material you've collected. Thank you, Miss Jonson.'

The boys trundled off in an untidy group towards the bus stop.

'Now, Symmonds. I think you and I had better have a talk,' said Mr Buxton.

'Haven't you got a lesson, sir?' asked John hopefully.

'No, as a matter of fact it's my free period before lunch and I've asked Miss Jonson to explain at school where I am. Now, I could do with a hot drink. How about you?'

Sitting opposite Mr Buxton in the little cafe, clasping a mug of tea and with a bun before him, John felt ill at ease.

'Now tell me,' said Mr Buxton, his eyes searching John's face, 'what exactly is happening? Tim Huggins said you were sick on

Wednesday. Then yesterday he came in saying you'd gone back for your history notes. Today his message seemed more confused. Sick again yesterday afternoon and then a dental appointment today. Unusually for your mother I've not received an excuse note nor has there been a telephone call.'

John reached for his bag.

'I have got a note, sir,' he said, feeling uneasy that he had put his mother in disrepute. He handed the note his mother had given him on Thursday morning. It was crumpled and damp. Mr Buxton opened the envelope and spread the letter out in the table.

'As I thought,' he said quietly. 'Sorry John was absent on *Wednesday*.' Mr Buxton emphasised the day as he read from the letter. 'No mention of Thursday or a dental appointment coming on Friday.' He looked questioningly at John. John lowered his gaze and quickly took a large bite of bun. He could not talk with his mouth full, he thought, and that would give him time to work out an answer.

But Mr Buxton was not waiting for a reply.

'I think it would be better if you could tell me the whole story, John. You see someone phoned school this morning. It was the lady at the corner shop in Rollestone Street. She said she had served a boy from Heron School yesterday and that he walked out of the shop and walked away from the town and back towards the river. It had worried her all night and she decided she ought to ring this morning.'

'Interfering old woman!' said John, fiercely brushing the crumbs of bun from his mouth.

'Not at all. She was a kindly soul and very worried. There's been reports of an odd character lurking around that lonely path by the river. The lady was trying to be caring. Now just suppose that it was you and you had found yourself in some difficulty. Who would have known? The school thought you were at home sick yesterday and your mother thought you were safely at school. No one would have missed you until home time at the earliest.'

'But I wasn't in any difficulty,' said John and then realised that he had given himself away. There was no use pretending any more. He pushed the crumbs of bun around his plate and finished the last dregs of tea. Mr Buxton sat silently. He didn't scold and neither did he ask any questions.

John didn't know why or how but he found himself telling Mr Buxton the whole story. The panic of his walk home on Tuesday, his fears for his mother, pretending to be ill, the hide-out behind the garden shed, the lies about the history test and the dental appointment, and finally the episode at the launderette. They even laughed together at the thought of John sitting draped in a beach towel at The Washing Well. There was an immense relief in telling the complete truth after all the deceptions of the last few days. Eventually John had finished and a silence fell between them again.

Mr Buxton felt into his jacket pocket. He pulled out a piece of paper and a ball-point pen.

'Now this may seem stupid, John, but I want you to write just two sentences on that piece of paper. One sentence is to be what you fear most at the moment. The other what you think you can most helpfully do at the moment.'

He pushed the paper and pen across the table. John needed no time to think. He wrote. 'I fear that something awful might happen to my Mum. I want to look after her and help her.' He folded the paper up and handed it back to Mr Buxton.

Mr Buxton read it and leant across the table, resting on his arms.

'Now let's look at this together. Is your Mum ill? Is there any reason whatsoever to think she might have an accident?'

John thought of his Mum always coping and trying to be perky even now when things were so difficult.

'No, I suppose she's OK.'

'So there's no reason for you to worry about her any more than there is a reason for her to worry about you is there?' Mr Buxton rocked back in his chair. 'We all feel frightened about things which might happen at some time in our life,' he continued. 'Very often these fears are imaginary, but in any case, living with a certain amount of fear is a pretty normal part of life. We all have to swallow anxieties some of the time. Life can never be completely free of risk.' He paused.

'Do you know, when I started at Heron School I was petrified.'

John's eyebrows lifted. Mr Buxton, the cool, calm, organised Mr Buxton, afraid? It didn't seem possible.

'It may sound stupid but I really was. You see it was only my second teaching post and the other job had been in a much smaller school. When I started at Heron for the first few weeks I would wake up in the middle of the night in a cold sweat.'

John couldn't prevent himself smiling. 'But what for? What was there to be afraid of?'

'Exactly. It was quite illogical but none the less real for that. I used to dream that I had lost my teaching notes for the lessons, that I couldn't find the classroom and then - and this was the worst dream of all - that you would all scream me down and I wouldn't be able to teach you at all.'

John laughed. 'But no one mucks around in your lessons, Mr Buxton, you know that.'

'Yes, I do. But I was afraid just the same. Afraid although there was no real cause for my fear. Can you understand?' John nodded. He felt a bit better just sharing his fears with someone else and for knowing that other people, even adults, sometimes felt as ridiculously frightened as he had.

'Now let's look at this other sentence - what you most hope for.' Mr Buxton turned back to look at John's second sentence. 'It's grand that you want to care for your Mum, especially just now. But do you think it will really help if you stay at home? Surely it would only worry her. She would worry about you missing your lessons, missing your friends, missing your life. I reckon if you asked her what would help her most she would probably say "Keeping on going". Doing the ordinary things, just as you've always done. After all, you can't really stay lurking around behind back sheds all your life can you?'

John twisted his hands uneasily. Had he been entirely stupid? What would everyone think of him now? But Mr Buxton's next words reassured him.

'What you're having to face demands a lot of courage. Doing what you did shows that you have a lot of courage already. It was kind to think you could care best by being near your mother, even if a bit misguided. But now you must have more courage. Courage to trust that all will be well. That you and your mother will be OK. Courage to trust life again.'

John looked out of the window at the heads of passing people and the tops of buses rounding the corner by the cafe. Mr Buxton stood up.

'I've been going on a bit. Better be getting back.'

John pulled his haversack over his shoulder.

'Sir?'

'Yes.'

'Will they all have to know about all this? The others in the class? The head?'

Mr Buxton drew in his breath. 'Don't worry about the other boys. I can satisfy their idle curiosity without letting them in on everything. That can be our secret. As for Mr Blackburn the head, and of course your mother - they'll have to know. You must see that it couldn't be otherwise. But I'll promise you one thing. I'm pretty sure I can guarantee that they won't mention it at all to you or anyone else unless - and it's a very big unless - you start your disappearing acts again. Is that a deal?'

'It's a deal, sir,' said John with a sigh of relief.

Mr Buxton steered him out of the cafe and they walked together towards the bus stop. Mr Buxton's words echoed in John's mind. 'Courage to trust life again.' He wondered if he had enough courage to try.

CHAPTER 7

It was one night in early November that John awoke with the sensation of drowning. He was in a boat being thrown from side to side amidst gigantic towering grey waves. As he lay in his bed trying to arouse himself from the nightmare, his mind was confused by the fact that he could still hear the sounds of the waves and the storm around him. He lay still trying to calm himself and shut out the sounds but still they persisted. He turned on the light in an effort to shake himself awake. The noise went on. Howling and shrieking, wailing and crashing. John gradually realised that although the boat and the waves were part of his dream, the sounds of the screaming wind were quite real. Mrs Symmonds appeared at the bedroom door.

'Are you awake, John? I'm not surprised. Can you hear the gale?' Fully alert now, John listened to noises he had only heard before as sound effects on the TV or radio. The wind moaned around the house, buffeting the windows so that they shook and shuddered in their frames. There was the sound of the dustbin clattering about on the concrete by the back door, and the higher tinkling shatter as milk bottles were bowled over and smashed by the front porch.

John got out of bed and went to the window. Outside the wind thundered through the trees, which creaked and groaned as they swayed first one way and then the other.

In the pool of light from his bedroom window a swirl of leaves lifted and turned on the grass like a whirling dervish. John watched in amazement. He had never seen something so invisible create such visible results. It seemed as if the wind was an unseen giant whose size could only be guessed at from the strength of his voice and the rushing of his breath. Mrs Symmonds dropped a dressing gown around John's shoulders.

'I think I'll pop downstairs and make a drink. We can hardly sleep with this racket going on.'

56

While his mother was in the kitchen, John noticed a light in Mr Flack's garden next door. He strained to focus more clearly. Who could be skulking around the garden at this time of night and in this weather? John turned off his light and pressed his face against the glass, trying to see better. Then he realised it was Mr Flack himself. What was he doing pottering around the garden now? John quickly worked out what the matter was. Further down the garden was a poplar tree. This tree was something of a joke and Mr Flack never tired of telling visitors the story of the poplar tree in his garden. He had cut a stout branch from a mature tree and put it in for a clothes post for Mrs Flack's washing line when they had first moved into the house almost thirty years ago. To their amazement, within a few years the clothes post had started to sprout, first twigs and then branches. Soon Mr Flack had been obliged to lop its ever-growing top branches each year and to provide Mrs Flack with an alternative prop for her clothes line.

Then in the spring of last year the poplar had failed to leaf. It had stood bare amidst the green of the pear, apple and cherry in the gardens and the massed hands of the horse chestnuts in the fields beyond. Mrs Flack had warned about the tree from the start.

'It's dead, Jack,' she would say. 'It will have to come down.'

But somehow Mr Flack had never got round to organising the felling. They had watched the fine lacework of its branches, delicate and fragile against the changing skies of that year. Mr Flack had seen the sense of his wife's words.

'That tree's dangerous,' she regularly repeated, and now, as he stood in the garden clasping his raincoat around him and hearing the wind howl through the top of the poplar, he was forced to concede that Mrs Flack had been right.

At first the branches spun and swung in the gale but gradually, as the wind persisted, Mr Flack could see the imperceptible swaying of the trunk. Finally the end came. There was a juddering and a sound like the rising cry of an animal as the tree fell through the air and finally thumped to the ground. It lay across Mr Flack's herbaceous border, its topmost branches crushing the fence and overlapping into the Symmonds' garden.

'Mum! Mum! Come quickly!' John yelled, but Mrs Symmonds was already behind him. Balancing the tray of tea on the chest of drawers, she peered out into the darkness.

'Oh, my goodness! I heard the crash as I was coming up the stairs. I was praying it wasn't the tree. Poor Mr Flack.'

Mr Flack had retreated to the far side of the garden as the tree fell. Now he cautiously approached the recumbent poplar as if it might still move. After a brief look, he pulled his mackintosh collar up and walked dejectedly back into the house.

John sipped the cup of tea which his mother had passed him and looked out through the lashing rain. There was no sign of any more movement in the garden next door and, when they had finished a second cup and nibbled at some rich tea biscuits, Mrs Symmonds and John decided to try to get some rest despite the continuing storm outside.

The following morning was clear and bright. The air was completely still and the sky a clear washed blue. It was as if nature was smiling this morning and denying any part in the howling tornado of the previous night.

Early in the morning, shortly after John had left for school, Mr Flack rang the front door bell of the Symmonds' house. He stood looking embarrassed.

'I've just come to apologise, Mrs Symmonds,' he began when the front door opened. 'About the tree.'

Teresa Symmonds opened the door wide.

'Come in, Jack. Not so much of the Mrs Symmonds. You've always called me Teresa.'

'I suppose I'm just feeling that awkward. If my Joan says "I told you so" once more I swear I'll scream.'

Mrs Symmonds smiled. She could imagine how self-righteous her good friend Joan Flack could be in the face of such overwhelming evidence of her sound judgement about the tree.

'I really am sorry, Teresa,' the abject Mr Flack continued. 'I should have seen to that tree in the summer. Somehow it was part of the scenery and I just didn't get around to organising a tree feller. Now that gale's done the job for me and a fair amount of damage into the bargain.'

They walked through the hall and kitchen, Mrs Symmonds pulled on her wellingtons and they went to examine the fallen poplar. It had brought down about six feet of fencing as it fell and now lay pathetically across the rockery.

'Once we've cleared away the tree I'll put the fence back in no time - and I'll pay of course. I don't want you worrying about anything.' Mr Flack was his usual kind self. 'The difficulty is I can't saw through these larger branches or the trunk but there's a chap who lives a few roads away who's got a chain saw. He's a friendly sort of man and I thought I'd ask him if he could give me a hand. Would it trouble you if we worked in your garden one Saturday morning?'

'Not at all, Jack. Now just stop worrying about everything. You couldn't possibly have expected that we would have such strong winds so early in the winter,' Mrs Symmonds said reassuringly.

That evening Mr Flack telephoned to say that he had contacted the neighbour with the chain saw, a Mr Curtis, and that they would both be round about nine o'clock on Saturday morning if that was convenient. John overheard the conversation.

'Sounds good,' he said. 'I might be able to lend a hand.'

But when Saturday came John did not appear to help.

He was in his bedroom when he heard the voices by the back door. He recognised Mr Flack's voice then another male voice and then his mother's. He peeked out of the window to see the little group walking down the garden. But there was someone else. A girl in jeans and a green anorak with long fair hair. John looked on jealously. Why was she there?

He continued to watch through the window whilst they first lopped the side twigs and small branches off the fallen tree and then turned their attention to the larger boughs and finally the trunk. He listened to the whine of the saw and watched as the young girl piled the smaller branches into a heap for a bonfire. Mr Flack moved the heavier logs into a neat pile by the side of the garage.

Even when his mother called up to say they were having a break for coffee, John made some excuse not to come down. He felt strangely put out by the arrival of this man with a saw and the competent girl, though he couldn't work out why. John watched them working steadily all morning and by lunch time the job was all but finished. He heard them talking together in the kitchen below and then at last the clang of the side gate. Satisfied that the coast was clear he came downstairs ready for lunch.

'Why on earth didn't you come and help?' his mother asked reproachfully. 'We could have done with another pair of hands.'

John muttered an excuse about tidying up his bedroom. At last he asked as casually as possible what the girl had been there for.

'Oh! So that was the problem was it? That's Catherine, Trevor Curtis' daughter.'

'I don't see why she had to come,' John went on disgruntled.

'Well, Mr Curtis couldn't leave her at home,' said Mrs Symmonds.

'Surely she could have played with her dolls or helped her mother,' John retorted sarcastically.

'She hasn't got a mother. Her mother died. That's why she had to come. She's only eight and too young to be left at home alone all morning,' said Mrs Symmonds quietly but firmly. John looked up.

'You mean there's just him and her. No Mum or brothers or sisters?'

'That's right,' said his mother.

'Kind of like us?'

'Just like us.'

John let the news percolate through his mind. He remembered the slight figure of the girl in the garden and wondered about her.

CHAPTER 8

It felt as if the end of the Autumn term would never come and that
the preparations at school for Christmas had been going on for ever.
The classrooms were festooned with decorations made in the art
classes and, in the Main Hall, a huge decorated tree stood by a
display of Nativity figures made of papier mâché by the first years.
It was all enjoyable and fun, but somehow this year John felt apart
from all the noisy jollity and exuberance. In the town, the shops
were full of tinsel and gift wrapping, glitter and baubles. John had
made a couple of trips to do his Christmas shopping. He had bought
some hankies for his grandmother, a book about football for his
cousin Edmund, and a poster of a cat for his cousin Hannah. Aunt
Evelyn and Uncle James had proved more of a problem but he had
finally decided on a joint present of a box of spicey biscuits. After
a lot of thought he had chosen a tiny china ornament of a basket of
flowers for his Mum. He wrote his cards for his friends at school.
The boys in the class did not exchange presents, unlike the girls who
seemed to spend their entire time before Christmas buying gifts for
every other girl in the class.

The last day of term arrived. There was always a final carol
service for the whole school in the large hall. Mr Blackburn the
headmaster addressed them all.

'And so the Staff and I would like to wish you all a wonderful
Christmas holiday. We hope you will have a really good time with
your families and come back safe and sound and ready for the next
term's work.'

There was a slight groan. No one wanted to think of next term's
work at the moment. The children burst out from the school like ants
scurrying from a disturbed nest. They rushed out from the doors
laden with sports kits, bags, models made during the term, and a

hundred and one other possessions dangling from their hands and shoulders or tied precariously to their bags. On the bus John and his friends sang all the alternative versions of the Christmas carols they knew until the bus slowed at the stop near his road. He slapped his friends on the back, made a few last jokes to Tim and, with a final shout of 'See yer!', jumped off the platform before the noisy party continued on its route.

Alone, John turned into the street towards his home. Dark was already closing in and there were lights at most of the windows. As he reached his own house he saw his mother already in the hallway. She had that bright look on her face which to John always seemed false, as if she was pretending a gaiety she did not feel.

'Come and see,' she said. She took John into the lounge. There in the corner stood a Christmas tree which was planted in a tub covered in red crêpe paper and gold tinsel.

'I got Mr Flack to dig it up from the garden as usual. It was too heavy for me on my own.'

John tried to look pleased. That evening he and his mother decorated the tree with all the familiar ornaments which had been collected over the years. Tiny wooden angels, white swinging candles, gaudy crystal balls which reflected the light, and of course handfuls of shining tinsel draped over it all. It looked magnificent when they had finished and John said so, hoping that he sounded cheerful. Inside he was feeling desolate. There were just two days until Christmas day. He found himself wishing it was all over. His grandmother and Auntie Evelyn had both invited them to stay with them for Christmas but finally they had decided to spend Christmas at home. It had seemed the right decision at the time but now doubts crept into his mind. Home seemed the only place to be at Christmas but would it feel like home now, he wondered? Would Christmas with just the two of them seem like Christmas at all?

*   *   *

Teresa Symmonds stood at the kitchen window and looked out at the dawn sky. It was streaked with grey and pink and that wonderful duck-egg blue which is especially the colour of sunrises and sunsets.

'It is Christmas day,' she said to herself. She had been unable to sleep and had got up early to prepare everything. There was not much to prepare. She had decided on the luxury of a piece of steak each. A turkey or even a chicken would have been ridiculously large for just the two of them. Carrots, sprouts, parsnips and potatoes were peeled and ready. The raspberry meringue was in the fridge, John's choice as he did not like Christmas pudding. Now the day lay ahead of them, long, quiet and interminable. Teresa looked down at the photograph she had carried downstairs from her bedroom. The man's face looked back at her, smiling, enigmatic. Strange, she pondered, to think that her whole world had changed in such a short space of time.

'How shall we get through today without you, Peter?' she whispered. There was a sound of movement upstairs. Teresa pushed the photograph into her apron pocket and, with a sharp intake of breath, turned to meet John.

'Happy Christmas, darling,' she said brightly, holding out her arms affectionately.

'Happy Christmas, Mum,' John replied pushing a parcel into her hands. Teresa undid the paper and held up the tiny ornament with obvious delight.

'Oh, John!' she exclaimed. 'It's beautiful. Oh, darling, you shouldn't have - these ornaments are so expensive. I shall put it on my dressing table.'

John flushed with pleasure. It was the first time he had bought his Mum's present without discussing his choice with anyone. Now Mrs Symmonds was leading him by the arm into the lounge.

'Come and have your presents. They're all under the tree.'

The two of them knelt on the floor, unwrapping the parcels. Mainly they were for John, but there were also a few for Mrs Symmonds too. John had a new football strip from his Mum together with a jumper, a book and a stocking full of tiny presents: A new rubber and pencil, a quiz book, a pack of cards and other stocking fillers. There was a model to make from Auntie Evelyn and Uncle James, some accessories for his railway set from his cousins, and from his grandmother, a huge box which proved to be a new board game.

'Great!' cried John as he pulled the new game from the wrapping. 'Just what I wanted.' He browsed amongst the contents of the box. Small bright counters and a large board marked out ready for play. There was also an instruction sheet with the rules.

Mrs Symmonds and John had a Christmas breakfast of grapefruit and toast by the fire. When they went to the door to fetch the milk for breakfast they discovered two more little parcels left on the doorstep: A bowl of planted hyacinths for Mrs Symmonds and a box of assorted toffees for John. They were both from the Flacks with a little note. It said 'Thinking of you especially at Christmas.' John looked out of the window. He knew the Flacks had already left early to spend the day at their daughter's. The street was deserted. There was none of the usual coming and going of working days. A strange silence was everywhere. He had never noticed it before. Christmas day had always seemed so noisy, so full of activity and, above all, so short. But this year, despite the tree and the lovely presents, it seemed a wasteland. They tried to fill the morning with activity. They had a game with John's quiz book, examined all their presents again together and even went for a walk through the empty streets into town. Even with all these distractions, they had still finished Christmas lunch, and washed and dried up by three o' clock.

'I suppose we could see what's on television,' said Mrs Symmonds, 'and then what about that game your granny gave you?'

John faltered. Looking at the instructions that morning he had read: 'A game for three or more players'. He hadn't thought of the number of players when he had put the game on his Christmas list.

'Perhaps another day, Mum,' he said, hoping she wouldn't notice the problem with the game. Another day he could ask some friends around to play. Not on Christmas day. No one would want to come today.

But just at that very moment someone did come. There was a quiet tap on the door. Surprised, even startled, Mrs Symmonds went to answer it. John followed her and looked out through the frosted glass panelling of the door where he could see the hazy figures of two people, a large person and a child. Mrs Symmonds opened the door. There stood Trevor Curtis and his daughter, Catherine.

'Why, it's Mr Curtis!' said Mrs Symmonds.

Mr Curtis was shifting uneasily from one foot to the other and when John looked at Catherine he noticed that her cheeks were stained and she looked as though she had been crying. Mr Curtis cleared his throat.

'We wondered if you would like to share something with us,' he stammered. Catherine held out her arms and then they noticed that she was carrying a large round tin. Balancing the tin against her, she prised open the lid. Mrs Symmonds and John peered into the tin. Inside was something like a Christmas cake. The icing was watery, and red and green colouring had merged into each other to give the cake a messy and somewhat grubby appearance. In the middle a rather pathetic Father Christmas tilted to one side.

John looked up with relief.

'Thanks, but we've already . . .' He did not finish the sentence as Mrs Symmonds suddenly interrupted, rather unnecessarily loudly John thought.

'Why, Catherine! It's lovely! Do come in. How kind of you to bring your cake to share with us.' Catherine stepped inside still looking nervous and hesitant.

'I tried to make it like . . . but the icing all went . . . and then . . .'

Mrs Symmonds made comforting noises, took the cake from her and then helped her off with her coat.

'John, show Mr Curtis and Catherine into the lounge and then come and help me with the cups and plates,' she instructed.

John ushered Mr Curtis and Catherine to a seat and then ran furiously to the kitchen.

'Mum!' he exploded. 'We've got your lovely cake. Have you seen her cake. It looks awful. Really, Mum, it will make me throw up.'

'Now, John, there's no need to dramatise. You can see she's upset. Of course we'll eat a piece of her cake. I promise you can have a slice of mine when they've gone.'

Mrs Symmonds put a doiley on her best pink plate with the roses around the edge and placed Catherine's cake in the centre. When she carried it into the lounge, Catherine's face lit up.

'It looks much better now,' she enthused. John even admitted afterwards that it tasted alright. Over the cake and tea, amidst the chatter of John showing Catherine his presents, Mr Curtis leant across to Teresa Symmonds.

'Thanks for saving the situation. She was so upset and you had mentioned that you were on your own for Christmas when I came to saw up that tree. I hope you didn't mind us arriving out of the blue but, to be honest, it's been a life saver,' he whispered.

'Perhaps for us too,' smiled Mrs Symmonds as she watched

John explaining to Catherine how he would assemble his new model.

When the teapot had been drained Mr Curtis stood up.

'Well, we must leave you to your evening,' he said. John looked startled. The excitement of showing his presents and the company had made it suddenly seem like Christmas. He didn't want them to go.

'But, Mum, can't we play my new board game? I know they'd like that.'

Mrs Symmonds paused.

'Well, we don't want to intrude,' Trevor Curtis said.

'But, Dad, it's only early,' pleaded Catherine. The two adults hesitated then laughed.

'Well, as it's Christmas,' said Mrs Symmonds. John gave an ecstatic whoop.

'I'll wash up the cups and plates, you get the game ready, Mum,' he yelled triumphantly. Catherine jumped to her feet, running behind John to the kitchen.

'I'll wash, you dry,' said John, grabbing his mother's apron from its customary peg. He put it on then twirled around like a model on a cat-walk.

'How do I look?' He strutted across the kitchen, one hand on his hip, the other behind his head. 'John is wearing the latest model in aprons,' he intoned in a 'posh' voice. Catherine doubled up with laughter. John, pleased to have an appreciative audience, warmed to his part. 'This version has wide straps for comfort,' he hitched the straps of the apron on his shoulders, 'and a useful pocket for knick-knacks.' He plunged his hands into the pocket. His hand came across something papery and shiny. He pulled it out and stopped frozen in his tracks. Catherine who had been laughing merrily, her earlier tears forgotten, came over and stood beside him following his gaze.

'Who's that?' she asked.

'It's a photo of my Dad,' said John trying to control his emotions.

'He looks very nice,' said Catherine quietly.

'He was,' said John simply.

'So was my Mum,' whispered Catherine. John heard the wistfulness in her voice. She knew what it was like, he thought, even if she was only a little girl.

CHAPTER 9

The Candlemas Fair in Wimbury was a symbolic event which marked the rising hope that winter was coming to an end. It came when the snowdrops were flowering in great green and white clusters around the trees, at that moment when the world seems poised on the brink of spring while still caught in the grip of winter. A hushed expectancy seemed to hang over the town as if its inhabitants were silently hoping that the noise and colour and music which the fair brought would trigger the arrival of the dancing days of daffodils and blossom, warm breezes and sunlight.

John had only been to the fair in the daylight when he was younger. For some reason he had never been in the evening when darkness closed in and the night lights came on. So he was overjoyed when Mrs Symmonds announced that Trevor Curtis had invited them to join him and Catherine on Tuesday evening to go to the fair.

'He'll pick us up tonight about seven o'clock after he's finished work,' Mrs Symmonds told John when he got home from school.

Punctual to the minute, Trevor Curtis arrived on the dot of seven o'clock. Catherine, bright-eyed and wrapped in woollen scarf and hat, could hardly keep still. They walked through the streets down the hill towards the market square where the fair was held. A mist hung around the buildings, hiding the top of the church tower at the end of the main street. There was a trickle of younger children wandering wistfully homewards with their parents, balloons attached to their pushchairs and their mouths sticky with toffee apples.

At the end of the High Street the distant music of the fair could be heard, but as they drew nearer the music was overwhelmed by the droning of the generators. Lorries had been parked, cabs outwards, forming a circle of vehicles around two sides of the square. Their trailers housed the generators which ran the electric rides. On the other two sides of the square were shops so that the fair was enclosed in a magic circle of its own. Once inside that ring John was captivated by all he saw and heard. The noise was amazing. Traditional fairground music vyed with blaring pop tunes, whilst above all could be heard the shouting of the stall holders and the tinkling of the bells on some of the rides.

The rides! When John had visited the fair in the daytime as a small child only the rides for the younger children had been operating. Then he had thought it marvellous to ride on the backs of giant ladybirds, to pretend to drive a fire-engine and ring its bell, or to hoot the horn on the racing car as it turned on the roundabout. But now he realised that the daytime fair was like an engine just ticking over that only roared into life at night. At night it flashed with a million coloured lights, the whirling and turning rides were its myriad parts and it caught up the screams and shouts of all the people in its roar.

They were jostled through the crowds past the boxing booths, the man at the entrance, microphone in hand, enticing the crowd to go inside to watch the contest. They watched with amusement as the trucks of the ghost train trundled out of the tunnel with the occupants screaming, eyes tightly shut. They craned their necks to see the swinging carriages of the Big Wheel and the twirling umbrellas of the Waltzers. They strolled past sweet stalls: Stalls hung with pink clouds of candy floss, walking sticks of Smarties, and lollipops of multicoloured rock; stalls with neat piles of curled brown brandy snaps, nougat, slabs of pink and white coconut.

They meandered and loitered by the stalls with competitions. They unsuccessfully tried to win a gaudy green dinosaur by rolling ping-pong balls. They hooked ducks on a rod and chose prizes from the central pyramid of cheap plastic necklaces, yoyos and plaster ornaments. They stood entranced, watching the barrel organ with its pipes and cymbals, its tinkling figurines waving Union Jacks. Their last ride of all, once they had exhausted themselves on the dodgems and helter skelter and the waltzers and had spent their entire pocket money on the games, was to go all together on the old-fashioned roundabout.

The carriages of this roundabout were gilded with large carved painted figures standing before and behind each carriage like a

figurehead on the prow of a ship. The colours were as vivid as the colours of a painted canal boat and all the woodwork, for it was wood not metal, was decorated with painted leaves. A board beside the roundabout told its history: How it had been sold to America during the last century but now had been returned and restored. The roundabout used to be driven by steam but now it was driven by electricity. Mrs Symmonds sat in the back of the carriage with Mr Curtis, while John and Catherine sat in the front. The operator in his black peaked cap blew his whistle and they were off. Just as they began to move, some school friends of John's appeared running along beside the roundabout. They cupped their hands to their mouths to shout above the noise to him.

'Hey! Symmo! John!' They waved, hurling their arms above their heads. 'Is that your girlfriend?' they shrieked, pointing at Catherine.

John blushed and nearly fell out of the carriage in his efforts to deny this. He had to stop such a rumour at once. What could he say?

'Of course not, stupid. It's my sister, my sister,' he yelled back as the roundabout gathered up speed.

'I wish I was your sister,' said Catherine but, leaning backwards and waving to his friends, John was not listening.

* * *

As February passed into March the Curtises became regular visitors. Trevor Curtis dug the heavy soil of the vegetable patch with John and gave the lawn its first cut of the year. They often had meals together and Catherine would try to impress them all with her efforts at baking. The months slid swiftly towards Easter. Auntie Evelyn had written asking John and his mother to stay for the holiday.

'We missed seeing you at Christmas,' she wrote, 'and we do worry about you both. Why don't you stay for a week? Hannah and Edmund would be company for John and you could have a rest.'

'I think we ought to go,' said Mrs Symmonds thoughtfully, passing the letter to John across the breakfast table. So they did. They packed their bags the first day of the Easter holiday and set off for Braebridge by bus and train.

As John had feared, the week had been thoroughly well organised by Auntie Evelyn. It wasn't that she wasn't kind, he reflected afterwards. It was just that she ran everything as if it was a school outing. Each day had an 'event' planned. A picnic with a treasure hunt, a healthy walk, a visit to an interesting museum, a day at a castle and so on. There was also the inevitable 'church crawl', when Auntie Evelyn took his mother to what she always described as 'a beautiful spot with this dear little church'. There John would wander about whilst his aunt walked, guide book in hand, exclaiming at old inscriptions or lifting carpets to look at ancient brasses. It was the same this Easter. On Easter Monday they set off for the church crawl. The church was in a sizeable village and when they entered, to their surprise, it was not empty. There was a choir practising.

Just inside the door a tall, slim, white-haired lady was busy watering the flowers around the base of the font. The church was full of flowers: window ledges, lectern and pulpit were all festooned in the yellow and white of spring. There was a leafy scent which mingled with the smell of polish, and gave the feeling of cleanliness and freshness.

'This choir comes every year on Easter Monday,' the white-haired lady explained. 'We're lucky enough to have a very good organ, the gift of some wealthy lord of the manor some years ago. We have a concert of Easter music every Easter Monday. Very beautiful.'

She looked at John and his cousins.

'Would you like to see the Easter Garden?' she asked.

She led Edmund, Hannah and John across the church. In a corner of the nave a hill had been made of stones and rocks covered in moss. On the top were three empty crosses. To the left at the bottom of the hill a cave had been made out of stones. A round stone, like a door, was rolled to one side and inside on the ground was a tiny roll of white linen. At the back some children had painted houses to represent the city of Jerusalem. Tucked in the moss were tiny jars full of primroses, grape hyacinth and primulas. It portrayed the whole story of Easter.

Hannah and Edmund bent down to look closer but John's attention was drawn by the music and he moved away. He had never heard such a lovely sound as the choir's singing. He crept closer to the choir stalls and slipped into a pew at the side. He could see the concentration on their faces as they worked to perfect each phrase. At last the choir master seemed satisfied.

'Right, we'll try just the first and last verses please.'

The organist began and John listened to the soaring sound. The words were clear as cut glass.

'Now the green blade riseth from the buried grain,
Wheat that in dark earth many days has lain;
Love lives again, that with the dead has been:
Love is come again,
Like wheat that springeth green.

'When our hearts are wintery, grieving or in pain.
Thy touch can call us back to life again,
Fields of our hearts that dead and bare have been:
Love is come again
Like wheat that springeth green.'

John sat still when the last sounds had died away. Something in the poetry of the words and music had touched him.

At the end of the week Auntie Evelyn, Hannah and Edmund took John and Mrs Symmonds back to the station by car. Standing on the platform waiting for the train, John realised that he was glad to be going home. Although grateful for the company of his cousins and the well-intentioned kindness of his aunt, he was glad to be going back, back to their own home, a home where he and his Mum were beginning to feel comfortable again. The train trundled along the platform, drowning the last words of his aunt as she hugged Teresa to her. John was looking at the engine. It had a brass name plate on it. The name of the engine was *Courageous*. John smiled to himself as he waved goodbye.

CHAPTER 10

Teresa and John sat on the wooden seat in the garden under the last blossoms of the mock orange tree. Overhead the house martins swooped and dived in the fading light of the June evening. Teresa smiled.

'Your father used to call the house martins the Red Arrows of the bird world,' she said to John as they watched the acrobatics in the sky. They gazed in amazement as the birds turned, sheering upwards in flight with such incredible power and grace.

'I love this garden,' Teresa said half to herself.

'Me too,' said John.

'I remember when your Dad and I first moved to this house,' she continued. 'You were just a tiny baby, John. The house was in a dreadful state; dirty, with paint peeling off the window ledges outside and inside every single room needed decorating.'

'How about the garden? Was that in a state too?' John asked.

'The garden! The garden was derelict. Knee high in weeds. You couldn't tell the flower beds from the lawn. How we worked, your Dad and me! First we tackled the house, scraping off old paper, painting and mending. Then we set about the garden.'

'You must have worked dreadfully hard,' said John. He had only ever known the garden when it was well cared for with beds full of flowers and a vegetable patch lovingly tended.

'Oh, we did.' Teresa bit her lip, remembering the fun she had with her husband. 'We tried to plan it so that each season had something of colour and beauty to show. First the snowdrops.'

'Dad used to call them "Fair Maids of February",' John murmured.

'Then the crocus, daffodils, iris and polyanthus.'

'And now the orange blossom and the first of the roses. You really thought it all out, didn't you?'

'Yes - and then your Dad grew those lovely chrysanthemums and his favourites, the Michaelmas daisies, for the autumn. We had it all worked out.' Teresa sighed. John glanced at her quickly and sensed within himself a tremble of anxiety. He realised how difficult it had been for his mother since his Dad had died. He found himself wondering about Trevor Curtis and his Mum. He knew that they liked each other. He had been turning it over in his mind as he had watched their friendship develop during the last months. He quite liked Catherine and they certainly had fun when they were together. Trevor had helped his Mum too. He had dug over the garden and mended the washing machine when it went wrong last winter, and best of all, Trevor had made his mother laugh again. A few weeks earlier he remembered his mother had tentatively raised the possibility of her getting married to Trevor. The idea of his mother being married to someone else, even someone he liked as much as Trevor Curtis, disturbed John. He looked at her sideways and knew she was thinking about it now.

'I can't see why you have to get married, Mum,' he said. 'Why can't we go on just as we are - having meals together and going out for outings.'

Teresa looked down. How could she explain to John how she felt about Trevor, how she had longed for company, for someone to share her worries and hopes with, someone to understand - something she had never expected to find again.

'It just seems so much simpler. It's a bit silly running from one house to another.'

'But he wouldn't expect me to call him Dad, would he?' asked John.

Teresa put her hand on John's.

'Of course not. You could just call him Trevor or whatever you thought best. I don't expect Catherine would want to call me Mum either.'

John pondered on what it would be like having a sister.

'I suppose Catherine would sleep in the spare room,' he said aloud.

'Well, John, that's the next thing I have to talk to you about,' said Teresa. 'If we got married we thought it would probably be best if we moved to the Curtis' house. It's a bit bigger and has four bedrooms. It's still near enough for you to go to the same school and . . .'

John leaped up.

'Move! Move away from our house!'

He had prepared himself for the fact that his mother might re-marry but he had never ever contemplated having to move. Teresa gulped. She hadn't expected such a violent reaction.

'I'm not moving!' shouted John. 'Either they come here or I don't come. I'll, I'll . . .'

His voice trailed away as he realised how limited the choice of what he could do was.

'I'll go and live with Gran!' he shouted as he half-ran, half-stumbled from the garden and raced to his room.

He slammed the door of his bedroom and flung himself onto his bed. How could he move from here? His bedroom was somehow part of him. The shelves were stacked with his books and comics, his favourite posters were on the walls, his model aeroplanes suspended from the ceiling. It just wasn't fair. He couldn't be expected to leave it all. It wasn't that he didn't like Trevor. He was kind and good fun. Trevor and Catherine could join him at his house but they mustn't expect him to move to theirs. It was impossible. When had Mum said the wedding might be? Mid-August? That would mean moving this summer perhaps. John curled himself into a tight ball. Everything seemed so incredibly difficult.

The door of John's bedroom swung violently open. His mother stood there, her hands on her hips.

'Now, just wait a minute, young man! What do you think you are doing running away in the middle of a conversation and slamming doors? Just you wait and think a minute.' Her voice was high and shrill and John could see the colour in her cheeks.

'You don't want to move! You this, you that! Do you suppose that you're the only one to have feelings?' Mrs Symmonds stepped into the room wagging her hand menacingly in front of John's face. John cowered back on the bed. He had never seen his mother so angry before, she was normally so quiet and gentle-mannered.

'How do you think Trevor Curtis feels? How do you think Catherine feels? Don't you think they need consideration too? Do you suppose it's been easy for me trying to cope this last year? Do you think there aren't worries trying to pay the bills and keep the house and garden looking decent? I've tried so hard, so hard and now . . . and now . . .'

The tirade of words stopped. Mrs Symmonds stepped forward and sat crumpled on the end of the bed and, to John's absolute horror, she began to cry.Tears spilled down her face and her shoulders shook as her breaths came in halting gasps. John swung his legs off the bed and moved towards his mother. He put his arms around her to comfort her and then found that he was crying too. Shuddering sobs shook his body. His nose was running and his eyes felt swollen and hot. In his weeping were all his hopes and fears. He cried for what he had enjoyed and now lost; for what he had hoped for and now seemed impossible; for what was to come and yet still, despite everything, felt unacceptable. He cried that he had not used all the opportunities to be with his Dad and that these chances had now gone. He cried at the thought of the years ahead and of the plans he would not be able to share with his father. He cried as he felt the grief of his mother as her tears mingled with his. At last the crying subsided and they both sat still and exhausted.

'It's no use, John. I can't go through with it all,' Mrs Symmonds said, trying to control her voice.

'But I thought you liked Trevor. Wanted to marry him. I thought that's what you wanted,' John said gently. Mrs Symmonds shook her head slowly.

'It's not that. Trevor's fine. He's kind and he's good, and I'm sure he'd try to be thoughtful and kind to you which is what matters most to me. It's just . . .'

'Just what?' prompted John.

'Just the thought of moving. Leaving here. There are so many things I love about this house. So many memories. I just can't bear the thought of leaving it all behind. Why, oh why did everything have to change?'

John passed his mother his grubby handkerchief and she blew her nose. He got up and stood by the window looking down at the garden.

'But it has changed, Mum. Things can never be the same again - they can't be, can they? Not anymore. We've got to leave it all behind. Haven't we? Really?'

He looked at the mock orange bush they had been sitting beneath just a short while before.

'Things change like the garden you and Dad planted. I suppose there are seasons in our lives too just like the garden.'

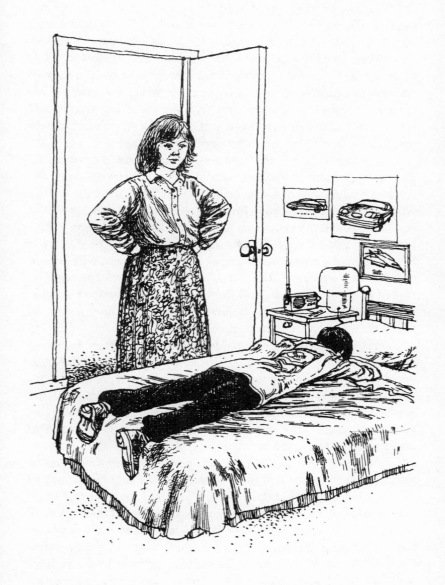

Teresa came and stood beside him. She put her arm around his shoulder.

'We'd be moving together, Mum' said John and he gave her a hug. 'It would be like a new start. You know the Curtis' house isn't that bad. There's a nice garden with loads of roses - you like roses.Then the kitchen has a lovely view and there's a spare bedroom like you said.' John found that he was building up an encouraging picture of moving to the other house, forgetting in his efforts to comfort his mother that only a short while ago he himself had been refusing to move. It was as if in sharing their tears and pain together he had found a new strength and courage.

So, when Trevor Curtis and Catherine arrived the following Saturday afternoon, it was John who shepherded his mother into the car and walked arm in arm around 57 Elm Tree Road suggesting where her favourite pieces of furniture could go and pointing out the benefits of the large bathroom and the spacious utility room. Then in the weeks that followed it was John who worked so hard helping his mother pack china in newspaper and fill tea chests with books, and take down pictures. He was so busy that he hardly noticed the end of the summer term and the beginning of the long August holidays and could scarcely believe it when his mother remarked that it was the last week in their old home.

Teresa, Trevor, Catherine and John had discussed how the move and the wedding were to be organised at great length. They had decided that the wedding would be mid-week on Wednesday 12th August. On the Tuesday evening, Trevor would pick John and his mother up and drive them to The White Hart, a large hotel in Wimbury where John and Teresa would spend the night. The wedding would be in the old church at the end of the High Street at 12 o'clock the next day. After the wedding, Teresa and Trevor would go away for a few days on a honeymoon; Catherine would go to Trevor's parents and John to Teresa's mother, and then on Friday they would collect John and Catherine. They would then have the weekend together at their 'new home' and move the last of the furniture during the last weeks of August. Some of the furniture from both homes would have to be sold to make room for everything and they didn't want to rush things and make the wrong choices.

Tuesday 11th August seemed to arrive so swiftly. John and Teresa had their cases packed and ready by the door. They had checked all the windows were shut and the doors locked. Trevor's maroon car slid quietly up in front of the house.

'This is it, darling,' said Teresa, unable to conceal her tears.

'Come on, Mum. No turning back now.'

They put the cases outside the front door and John slammed it behind them. Trevor picked up the case and walked ahead to the car whilst Teresa and John walked behind. But when they got to the gate they both turned. Whatever there was to look forward to there was also much that would never be forgotten. They got into the car and drove off.

CHAPTER 11

After weeks of unbroken sunshine the wedding day dawned dull and rainy. Not just a shower but torrential rain with not a break in the leaden sky overhead. John and his mother had breakfast in their hotel room. John had a cooked breakfast but Mrs Symmonds ate practically nothing, he noticed.

At half-past ten, Auntie Evelyn and Uncle James arrived with Hannah and Edmund. Edmund was wearing a grey suit and a tie and Hannah had a long pink dress on and was complaining loudly that she was freezing. They had coffee in the hotel lounge and then Auntie Evelyn went upstairs to help John's Mum put on her wedding suit. By quarter to twelve they were all assembled, waiting for the car to take them the short journey to the church. Teresa Symmonds was wearing a pale cream suit with a spray of flowers on the lapel and a white hat. She clutched a tiny bag with flowers on too.

'You look lovely, Teresa,' said Uncle James, tucking her hand under his arm. 'Now come on, everyone. The car has arrived.'

The next hours seemed to John on reflection to be a blur of people and movement. The journey to the church, the service in the wide airy chancel with the dark wooden carvings behind the altar; The party back at the hotel, the confetti and the waving-off of the bride and groom; Then more gathering of cases and packing into Uncle James's car, John squeezed next to Granny with Hannah perched on Granny's knee; The drive out of town and through country lanes to Granny's house, a massive tea together and then more goodbyes as Auntie Evelyn, Uncle James, Hannah and Edmund left for home.

Granny had then insisted on a bath and had brought John a cup of hot chocolate to his bedroom. She sat on the edge of his bed chatting until she thought he was sleepy.

'Now are you sure you are comfortable, dear?' she said, patting the pillows yet again. John suddenly wanted to be alone. He closed his eyes and grunted, hoping that Granny would leave him in peace. He lay back, pretending to be relaxed and on the point of falling asleep. At last Granny went, shutting the door quietly behind her. John waited until he had heard the last footstep on the stair and the kitchen door close and then he sat up. He lay back on the pillows. There was a feeling of anti-climax like the end of an exhausting football match which had finished in a draw. He felt neither exhilaration nor disappointment, just a general lethargy and lack of energy.

'So what now?' John thought. The pillows felt incredibly uncomfortable and he punched them viciously. There was something hard beneath the pillow. He fumbled behind him and at last pulled out a parcel wrapped in blue and yellow striped paper with a small card attached. John flipped the card over. 'From Auntie Evelyn to my nephew John' it read. John felt the parcel expectantly but then put it down on the coverlet with a sigh. He could tell it was a book from the shape. Another book. Auntie Evelyn always gave him books, it seemed. True, she tried hard enough to find something which was connected with his interests. John remembered there had been a book about dinosaurs when he had been about eight, then there was a grand book about angling when he had first begun fishing. But there had also been carefully chosen stories which John felt he ought to read but somehow never enjoyed. No doubt this was another such story intended to occupy his time during these three days. He glowered at the parcel and then was ashamed at his ingratitude. Auntie Evelyn always meant well. Eventually curiosity got the better of him and he leant forward and picked the parcel up. He peeled the Sellotape back carefully so that the paper would not be torn. He unfolded the paper but inside was not the usual printed book he had expected. The book cover looked like leather with a fine gold leaf pattern around the edge. John turned the first page. 'John's Book' was written in careful red print. Then John noticed a folded note had slipped out from beneath the heavy cover. It read:

'My dear John, a long time ago you asked me about your family. Well, I didn't forget and I have managed to find out as much as I can and even to unearth some old photographs too. I have stuck them in this book together with a copy of the family tree as far as I can work it out.'

John turned to the book. On the first page was a carefully printed family tree.

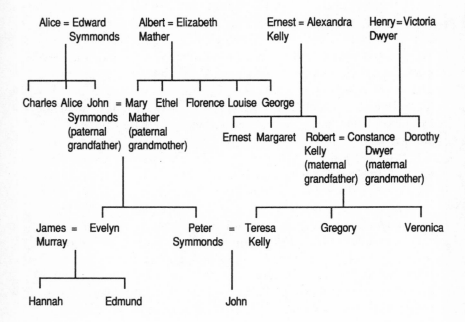

Then came some photographs neatly pasted in and labelled. There were black and white photographs of his Dad's father and mother and his Mum's parents. There was a colour photo of Auntie Evelyn, Uncle James, Hannah and Edmund on holiday. There were even a few sepia photographs of his father's grandparents, John's great-grandparents. His great grandfather wearing a striped suit stood posed with his hand on the back of a hard-backed chair in which his great grandmother sat demurely with her hands in her lap. He turned over the pages recognising some of the relatives and looking with curiosity at those he knew only by name: Great Auntie Florrie, Great Auntie Louise, Great Uncle George. There were some colour photographs of himself as a baby, as a toddler and in his school uniform. There too was the photograph of his father and Aunt Evelyn with their parents which John recalled looking at with Aunt Evelyn on the day of his father's funeral. Fascinated, he turned each page slowly until he came to about three-quarters of the way through the book where the photographs stopped. Paperclipped to the top of this page was a tiny note. It said simply: 'Have you read to the end of my letter? It's your turn to carry on the book now.'

Aunt Evelyn's letter! John had put it down in the excitement of seeing the photographs. He rummaged amongst the blankets and unearthed it again. Scanning the first few lines once more he continued reading:

'I have completed your family tree up to this day August 12th 19— but now it is your turn to carry it on. There will be difficulties and disappointments ahead but there will also be good times and laughter and, for someone like yourself who has courage and faith, I think it will be a fulfilling and worthwhile book. Look carefully at the family tree and photographs. You will see you are not the only one in your family whose mother has married again. Look at your Great Aunt Louise's photograph. That was her second husband. Her first husband was killed in an accident and the little boy beside them was his son. You're not the first one in the family to share your Mum with a stepsister either. Look at the photograph of your great granny's family. Henry and Victoria Dwyer were a kind-hearted and loving couple and the little girl sitting on the ground was looked after by your great granny although she wasn't really related at all.

Will you continue the book for us all? If you want to, your Granny has something which may help you to make the first step. Take courage, John. I'm sure all will be well.

Love from Auntie Evelyn.'

John turned back to the book. He found the photographs which Auntie Evelyn had mentioned and pored over them trying somehow to look into the minds of those people of long ago. Then, clasping the book to him, he walked slowly downstairs. His Granny was in the kitchen. She looked up as the door opened.

'Hello, dear. Can't you sleep? I was just going to make a cuppa. Would you like one?'

John held out the book towards her.

'Did you know about this, Gran?' he asked.

'Well, I must admit I did,' Granny replied. 'Your Aunt Evelyn has been pestering all the family for photographs for months - quite a pain she's been!'

'Auntie Evelyn said you would have something for me to help me go on with the book,' John went on.

'Ah, yes. You're right. She pushed something into my hand at the end of the reception. I put it in my bag. Now where did I put it?'

John felt his impatience rising as Gran looked first in the lounge, then in the hall and finally found the bag upstairs in her bedroom. She returned to the kitchen panting a little and searched in her bag for some while until she triumphantly pulled out a white envelope. It was labelled simply 'John'. John tore it open and out fell two photographs. One was of his Mum and Trevor alone at the wedding and the other was of Mum, Trevor, John and Catherine at the reception. Auntie Evelyn must have taken them on her polaroid camera especially.

'Have you got any glue, Gran?' John asked.

'Well, I think so, dear,' said Gran. She opened a kitchen drawer and there amidst string and rubber bands, old paper bags and paper clips, they eventually found some glue.

'And a pen, please?' After more searching they found a pen, pencil and ruler.

John carefully wiped the kitchen table with a tea towel. He didn't want any drops of water or grease to spoil this book. He opened the book just past the middle next to the last photographs. Taking the ruler, he drew a neat line at the top of the page. Then he positioned the two photographs and carefully stuck them in. Next he drew lines underneath and labelled each photograph. Underneath the first he wrote:

Mum and Trevor on their wedding day. August 12th 19—.

Underneath the second he wrote:

Mum, Trevor, John and Catherine.

Then in block capitals at the top of the page he printed:

MY NEW FAMILY.

John made sure the ink was dry then closed the book carefully. He stood up and noticed that his Gran was standing by the stove quietly watching him as the kettle came up to the boil. On an impulse he ran into her arms. He felt two tears squeeze out of his eyes. But they were not tears of bitterness or even sorrow. They were tears of thankfulness, for suddenly he saw with a great clarity that endings could also be beginnings and that the pain and sorrow of change could lead to something new and full of hope. His Granny gave him a big hug but wisely did not mention the tears.

'Now, how about that cup of tea I was talking about?' she said.
'Could you fetch the two big mugs hanging on the dresser?'

John walked into the dining room and lifted the two mugs down
carefully. As he carried them back he could hear Granny singing to
herself. He recognised the tune and he paused in the doorway to
listen.

'Steals on the ear the distant triumph song,
 And hearts are brave again and arms are strong'

sang Granny as the kettle began to whistle for tea.

/